The Dandelion in the Glass

Mandy Stafford

DP
Dawn Print

Dedication:

To my daughter Rosie for her inspiration

Frank Beattie

CHAPTER ONE:

THE END OF IT ALL

Only death can bring such blessed relief.

- Sinclair Montgomery, *The Old Man in the Forest*, 1867.

It should have been room 13. The room to the left was room 12. The room to the right was room 14. But this was not room 13. It was room 12A. It was small, almost square and drab, oh so very drab. The walls were a shade of dull pale yellow and very much in need of a coat of fresh paint. This room was dominated by an old tubular metal-framed single-tier bed. The frame was pale grey and the paint was badly chipped. The bed sheets lacked colour too, but there had been no complaints about the comfort of the bed. Beside the bed there was a small cheaply made cabinet. There was no toilet in this room, but there was a shared toilet just across the corridor. The room had a small washbasin, set tightly into one corner and the cool fresh water from the tap was good enough to drink.

The room had a window and in sharp contrast to the inside of the building, the world outside was wonderful. There was a pleasant view of the lush green lawn which swept gently down to the River Merrick and the mature trees a short distance beyond. The blue sky was often, or so it seemed, peppered with bright white clouds, and growing against the wall of the building were climbing roses, which, in the right season, produced flowers of a deep red colour. The window faced the west and on evenings when the weather was agreeable there was a view of the setting sun.

This small room 12A was only just adequate for the needs of its only occupant - Richard Graham Mackenzie Stansfield.

Craigmark Hospital shared extensive grounds with another hospital, Knadger House, where there was an accident and emergency unit and a maternity wing, all kitted out with modern equipment.

Craigmark had a high security wing, but this room 12A was not in that part of the hospital. Stansfield was not dangerous. Depressed, sometimes; delusional, yes; a persecution complex, occasionally; but not dangerous, never dangerous; not Tricky Dickie Stansfield. The staff were sure that he wouldn't hurt anyone, not even himself. Stansfield was aged 33. He was just a little shorter than the average man. He kept his thin grey hair short and tidy. Stansfield had a bit of a pot belly from lack of exercise and he walked with a slight limp that looked like a swagger that was almost comical. His face was rather square and looked a little flat. He was neither handsome nor ugly. His nose line told that it had once been broken. It was his eyes that most impressed those who met Stansfield. They were steel grey, but they gave a look that seemed to be hypnotic and certainly penetrating. What secrets lay in the disturbed mind behind those cold grey eyes?

Stansfield liked to keep his hospital issue clothes neat. If he had been allowed to, he would have worn a tie every day. One thing he did wear every day was a medallion on a neck chain. It was rather like a small silver coin. On one side there was an image of a horseshoe and on the other that of a four-leaf clover. Stansfield habitually took his lucky medal off at night, but he wore it every day for luck, at least he did when he remembered to clip it round his neck.

Stanfield's face lacked anything that hinted of fun or happiness. Richard Graham Mackenzie Stansfield had little to be happy about.

Like so many other patients at Craigmark, he had a daily routine. Up in the morning, wash, shave, dress, breakfast, then a little free time, followed by some organised events, tea break, some medical checks and so on throughout the rest of the day. Sometimes, but not every week, there would be visitors with some form of group entertainment like a sing-song, a talk about the town or a demonstration on how to paint or draw. Stansfield did not care for this change to the established routine. He did not care to interact with the other patients or with people from the outside. He preferred to be on his own and to do things that did not mean that he was part of what the nursing staff liked to call 'the team.'

While others took part in such social activities, Stansfield preferred solitude. In good weather he would go for walks in the grounds. Mostly, however, Stansfield was in the habit of spending much of his free time watching films on television in the common room. He even had a small television in his own room. Television was about his only pleasure these days.

In reality Stansfield was an unhappy inmate. He was not quite sure when he had decided that he knew his brain was a bit foggy. It had always been a bit foggy. If he sat and concentrated really hard he could remember that even when he was a child his parents would ask him about events, usually unpleasant events, that he simply could not remember. His brain seemed to be able to erase all unpleasant memories, just rub them out of existence.

His parents…, yes mum and dad had always been there for him. They always seemed to be happy, always concerned about him, always pampering him. He had a brief image of his mum and dad smiling happily and giving him a present from under a Christmas tree. Christmas. Happy parents. Happy memories…. But he quickly pushed this memory away before it turned bad.

Stansfield wasn't quite sure when he had concluded that he actually cared that every boring day was exactly like the boring day before. He could not remember when he started being concerned that his memories nearly always seemed to end badly, like dreams he could not control. Maybe they were dreams. He was never quite sure; never sure of what was real and what was not.

But he could remember when he first thought that there was only one way out of the hospital, and it wasn't through the front door. It was evening and as he looked out of the window of his room 12A, he saw a glorious sunset with a long crimson streak along the horizon.

The crimson gleamed before his eyes in another half-remembered image, one of blood. This was a memory from his childhood, a memory he had locked up far away at the back of his mind. When he was about seven years old Stansfield was playing at the seashore. He found a glass bottle. He set it up on a pile of sand and threw stones at it. None of the stones hit the bottle, so Stansfield picked up a larger rock, walked up to the bottle and dropped the rock on it. An instant before he let go of the rock he had the idea that this was an incredibly stupid thing to do, but he pushed that idea out of his mind. The bottle exploded and a shard of glass flew past his foot leaving a white streak, which almost immediately turned a deep crimson colour. Stansfield saw the crimson trickle before he felt the pain.

There were screams and there were tears. There was a trip to Knadger House Hospital where his foot was cleaned, X-rayed and stitched. There were questions, sympathy, questions and more questions. The same questions, over and over again. Of course, little Richard would never have done anything quite so stupid as to drop a big rock on a glass bottle. So the story he told his parents and the nurses and anyone else who asked all those questions was that he was running in the sand and fell on the broken bottle. Later, Stansfield actually came to believe the version of events that he had created for himself. Now, for the first time he knew that he had two versions of that event in his head…. and for the first time since he was seven years old, he knew which was the true version.

As he remembered the reality of this almost forgotten seashore incident he had a flash of an idea… yet another crimson streak of blood, this time across his wrist. Yes, he could do it, with scissors perhaps. But, of course, Stansfield did not have access to scissors, so he put the thought of ending his own life out of his mind, at least for a while.

Sometimes Stansfield sat alone in his room and let his mind wander into that dangerous place called The Past. He fingered the medallion dangling from his neck and thought hard. He was in a shop with his school friend, Ben McCutcheon. Ben, yes, but everyone called him Butch (1). There were coins and medals, metal advertising boards, toys, all manner of things and many boxes sitting on shelves and on the shop counter. Butch distracted the man behind the counter and Stansfield took the medallion. He did not steal it because he liked it. He did not steal it because he wanted it. He stole it because it was the first thing his fingers clasped when the man behind the counter was not watching him. Of course, when mum and dad asked about the medallion with the horseshoe on one side and the four-leaf clover on the other, sweet little Richard told them he had bought it. Mum and dad.... Mum and dad... and he pushed that memory far away, into a dark place somewhere at the back of his mind.

Another boring day followed another boring day and Stansfield let his mind relax and drift but harsh thoughts, dark thoughts came to him. He tried to ignore them but they came back. Back and forth, in and out, like the tide on that seashore so long ago.

Stansfield was trusted to take his medication. But it was Stansfield who had other ideas. He started storing the little capsules of medicine, secreting them all around the dark recesses of his room, like memories stored in the dark recesses of his mind. He still had no conclusive plan to kill himself by taking all the medicine at the one time, not really. But it was an easier option than trying to steal scissors form… well, somewhere.

One morning, as Stansfield looked casually at the metal frame of his bed his mind drifted back to a time when he had his own room, his own bed…, a wooden framed bed, back at mum and dad's house. But mum and dad were in that memory and he did not want to think about them.

Stansfield began to wonder what other memories were locked up in his brain. At least they were better than the occasional thoughts of suicide which penetrated his mind. Occasional flashes came to him. Sometimes it was just a word that helped the memory to come up to the surface, sometimes a smell, or some object he had seen.

Sometimes he could concentrate for only a few minutes at a time with only vague fuzzy memories... like going into Hufton's newsagent's shop with Butch. He would talk to his mum because she worked there, and while he had distracted her attention Butch would steal sweets or chocolate. News! Yes, as Stansfield thought about the shop he thought about newspapers. Had he not been in the newspapers for something? What was it? Did it have something to do with trying to break into the old abandoned Dominie House near the Hudson Park? He was not quite sure.

At other times his thoughts came more quickly and in sharper focus. In this state of mind he could remember more.

But in general, it was like trying to remember a dream just moments after waking up. One minute it all makes sense and you are certain of everything, but the next you just can't remember what you were thinking... and you know that it is only the uncertainty that is real.

Stansfield had no friends. He sometimes chatted with a few of the other patients and some of the staff but there was no one he really wanted to talk to.

Every Sunday afternoon the hospital held a brief non-denominational church service with singing of hymns, a few prayers and a short sermon by the hospital chaplain, The Rev Mark Lucas from the local Dunmerrick Parish Church.

Stansfield did not attend these services. They reminded him too much of his childhood Sundays when his mum made him go to church and Sunday School each week, whether he protested or not.

One Sunday afternoon after the close of the service, Stansfield was sitting alone at a small table in the common area, not quite thinking about anything. A figure came by. It was The Rev Lucas. They occasionally had chats together, usually one-sided chats with the minister doing all the talking.

"Hello" Stansfield remarked dully. Even as he said it, he had an odd sensation. Did he really crave some company for the first time since he was a child? The minister paused and sat down across the shabby little table facing Stansfield.

"Hello Richard. How are you today?"

Stansfield did not respond to the question. Perhaps he was thinking about it or perhaps he had nothing more to say. Stansfield was always a bit slow when it came to things like dealing with other people.

The Rev Lucas always found Stansfield a little difficult to talk to but he tried hard.

"Did you ever go to church? Did you go to Sunday School?

Stansfield tried to remember. Sunday School. Yes, he had a vague memory of something like that. "There was a camp fire," Stansfield started vaguely in a weak voice and not looking at the minister.

A smile spread across the minister's face. He had won a response from Stansfield. That was good. "Ah, yes, Sunday School children always liked to go on camping trips."

Fire. Stansfield was already struggling with another memory.

"Me and Butch was up the glen one time. We was climbing on the old folly and the police lifted us (2). Said we was trying to set it on fire. We got done for that. Dad was angry... Dad..."

Stansfield had a memory of his father for just a moment, but he quickly suppressed it. He said no more and did not hear what the minister said. The Rev Lucas held his hand out and Stansfield shook it automatically before the minister left thinking that Stansfield's chubby hand had been a little too warm and rather dry.

Later that day, Stansfield could not quite get the image of the folly out of his head. It had something to do with the police... the police visiting the house, no not for the folly fire, for some other reason, but again he pushed the memory away and he wasn't even sure if the image that had bubbled up was a real one or one that he had created to cover up something else.

Over a period of a few days, Stansfield played two conflicting ideas against each other in his confused head. He had no reason to kill himself, not really, and he had a strange fascination with some of the ideas that had started to come back to him.

17

He had been staring out of his window thinking about nothing as usual when he saw a man on the lawn. This man was sitting on one of those big grass-cutting machines and was about half way between the building and the river. There was something familiar about it. Stansfield used to use one of those machines. He was sure of it. A memory formed round the uncertainty. He had one of those machines in the Hay Park, beside the Funmerrick Leisure Centre. Good name, Stansfield thought. The parks department had storage space in the building. Stansfield found himself inside the building. Yes his dad worked for the parks department. That's why Stansfield got a summer job there as well. But these memories upset him and he stopped looking at the grass-cutting.

Were they real memories, or were they just thoughts of what might have been; thoughts of something he had made up? Stansfield didn't know.

Some time later, while he was idly staring into a cup of orange juice another childhood memory surfaced from deep inside his mind.

He remembered hanging about with a group kids his own age at primary school. They were all about eight or nine years old. In an unpleasant situation, such as if someone had stood in dog dirt, one of the group would shout 'Hob' and they would all run off in different directions in mock terror (3).

Fun times! But again there was a twist in the case of Richard Graham Mackenzie Stansfield, as there always was. He had been picked as goalkeeper for a football match but on his first game his team was defeated 13-1. Stansfield was blamed by his team-mates for his bad goalkeeping and was shunned for a while. When he turned up, someone would shout 'Hob' and they would scatter in all directions. Ever since he had hated being involved in team sports. He became a loner. Stansfield had suppressed this particular memory for years.

Slowly, ever so slowly, Stansfield decided that he wanted to capture some of those thoughts or memories that he never seemed quite able to reach out and grab hold of, no matter how hard he tried.

The more he tried to concentrate, the more Stansfield's memories sharpened. The best memories came back to him when he was lying in bed awake in the quiet moments before sleep: His car stolen; stealing sweets from shops, a woman laughing at him, a cottage he once lived in, a haunted cottage, perhaps. He could never quite sort out his memories, never quite put them into any order. Sleep always caught up with him. It would be best, he decided, to write some of the memories down before they were lost forever.

And so, Stansfield asked for and was given a notebook and a rather blunt pencil. There was now another conflict in his mind. He wanted to keep the memories, but it was quite an effort for him to write anything at all. It reminded him of school and he had always hated school. School, yes. Stansfield and Butch McCutcheon took every chance they could not to go to school. They would take walks in Dunmerrick Glen, mess about in the Hay Park or the Hudson Park. It was all much better than going to school. He had never liked writing stories, never liked writing anything. He had never been good at it. But Stansfield was determined to remember as much as possible and get it all written down. For the first time in his life he wanted to understand himself.

He started trying to train his mind to remember things during the day when he would not lose them to sleep.

The memories usually came back to him in pictures, like images on a badly tuned television. Stansfield found that once he had an idea, if he could concentrate for long enough, then he could stretch a still image into a moving one. The hard bit was trying to get started.

He remembered standing by the shore of the loch about two miles from his home. He was angry. It was dark and he was watching the lights of two cars on the opposite bank. They stopped. One of the cars turned so the headlights came right across the water. The lights dimmed and went out. He shouted something. For all the good it would do he picked up a rock and threw it in the direction of the remaining car.

His anger from that moment returned and in an untidy scrawl he started writing his first memory on the first page of the notebook.

Over the next few days Stansfield discovered that if he tried too hard he could not remember properly. But, whenever he could, he wrote down things just as they came back to his mind. He thought that perhaps one day he would go over the notes and sort them all out.

At this time Stansfield started to seek company, companionship. Most of the people at Craigmark had friends and sat in groups. But then there was Roderick Wiseman.

Like Stansfield he was a loner. He enjoyed his own company. About the only person Wiseman ever spoke to was himself. He could see faces in everything, in the clouds, the trees, even stones. Wiseman was convinced that these faces were sky spirits, tree spirits, all manner of spirits and all watching him because he knew too much… but then again, like Stansfield, Wiseman lived at Craigmark.

Stansfield saw Wiseman sitting on a bench looking out across the lawn towards the river. He took his decision without further thought. He would try to become friends with Wiseman. After all, in their loneliness, they were kindred spirits. The only difference seemed to be that Wiseman, like so many others, wore his own clothes.

Stansfield, for reasons he could not quite remember, wore hospital issue clothes.

Wiseman was short, but heavily built. His hair was short and wiry and he had slightly bulging eyes. As Stansfield approached, Wiseman turned to look up at the sky.

Stansfield sat on the bench next to Wiseman. "Hello. How are you today," he asked in a passable impression of the way Rev Lucas had greeted Stansfield.

"I see you." Wiseman's voice was rather gruff. "I see what you're up to. Oh yes, turn your face away now that I've seen you... and your friend, too. Oh now you're pretending to kiss each other. Very nice, but I know what you are really doing."

Stansfield looked up at the sky and with a bit of imagination could just about make out two roughly head-shaped clouds.

"I see them too," Stansfield told Wiseman.

"No you don't," Wiseman snapped. "You're just saying that. I'm the only one who can really see them. I know what they are up to. You can't see them. You are just saying that. Go away."

Rejected again, like the little boy from the football team, Stansfield left, knowing that he would be a loner for the rest of his life.

Just thirteen days after he started keeping a notebook, a particular memory came back to him. At first it was a memory of a different hospital. His right hand reached up to his neck, but his medallion was not there. Somehow he had forgotten to put it on that day. As the fog around his brain continued to clear, Richard Graham Mackenzie Stansfield suddenly realised that the other place where he had been for years had not been a hospital at all.

He remembered exactly where he had been and why he had been there. Years of self-denial broke like a dam and a flood of memories overwhelmed his brain. Most of them were not pleasant memories.

It did not take many minutes for Stansfield to decide that the moment had come. He wrote his last memory in the notebook in an untidy scrawl:

Bowhouse My fault

He gathered all the tablets together, and poured some water into a plastic tumbler. He hesitated for only a second before swallowing the mix in one gulp. A few seconds later, he vomited into the washbasin. He could feel numbness creeping into his brain, a numbness that made his thinking out of focus.

Whatever he had expected, it wasn't this. Stansfield turned in desperation to the sheet on his bed, now thinking again of a plan he had thought about several times before but had always backed away from.

He wanted to work quickly, turning it into a noose. If he delayed, his brain would be numbed. He might never have another chance. He tore a strip from it then switched on his portable television to cover any noise. With just a little hesitation he opened his door slightly and tied one end of his noose round the door handle. He threw his sheet rope almost casually over the door. Then he clambered clumsily on to his chair and slipped the other end of his noose round his neck. With a groan Richard Graham Mackenzie Stansfield jumped to oblivion.

Now, the only sound in his room came from the voice on the television. "Now on BBC Scotland, *Arts*

Today profiles one of Scotland's leading young artists, Gemma Dusk."

Fifty miles from the mental health unit at Craigmark Hospital, in an opulent detached red sandstone villa, Gemma Dusk and her nearest and dearest settled down to watch the television.

CHAPTER TWO:

IN THE WAKE OF DEATH

Who among us can say that death is final?

- The Rev Aitken Heywood, *Book of Sermons*, 1899.

The formal investigation into the death of Richard Graham Mackenzie Stansfield at the age of just 33 was thorough. Police officers were called in and they treated the situation in the same way that they would treat a case of murder. The officers may have suspected suicide. Suicide may have been obvious to everyone, but the police and others involved in the investigation did their jobs professionally and thoroughly.

The corridor outside room 12A at Craigmark was sealed. For about 36 hours the patients who lived in adjacent rooms were moved elsewhere in the hospital. One officer logged everyone who went into the sealed area, and no one was allowed in without prior permission.

Stansfield's room, the oddly numbered room 12A, was, of course, the focus of attention. Forensic investigators arrived soon after it was sealed. Even before Stansfield's body was removed from this part of the hospital, it was checked and photographed. The forensic team took away samples of the remains of the tablets and the vomit that they found in the corner washbasin. They took away his home-made rope. They took the remains of the bed sheet and the rest of the bedclothes. They took a small collection of personal belongings from the bedside cabinet, including his notebook. The police checked the room for any stray fingerprints. They looked in every nook and cranny. Between the bedside cabinet and the wall, one of the officers found a thin flat medallion, like a small silver coin on a chain. They took the medal away as well. They examined the window and, of course, they examined the door.

Police officers spoke to everyone who had been on duty on the night of Stansfield's death and those who had been off duty. They wanted to know what the hospital routine was. They wanted to know everything about Stansfield, what medication he had been given; who liked him and who didn't. Then, at last, they left the scene to cross check and study all the evidence and to write up their reports.

The suicide of one of the patients, and the subsequent fuss that was created by the investigation, had caused quite a stir among the other patients and the staff at Craigmark, but once the tape barriers had been removed and the investigators had left the building, the hospital quickly returned to its usual settled routine.

No one on the staff had any doubt that Stansfield had died at his own hand without help or influence from anyone else. They waited patiently for the official report to be published.

Stansfield's death attracted little public attention. There was a single paragraph at the bottom of a column of more important news on page 22 of the weekly *Dunmerrick Herald* nine days after he died. All it did was record the fact that Richard Graham Mackenzie Stansfield, 33, had died following an incident at the mental health unit at Craigmark Hospital. There were no suspicious circumstances. An investigation was under way and a report would go to the procurator fiscal.

That was all. That was all that could be said about the whole life and death of a man. It gave no hint of what kind of incident had occurred in the hospital, but anyone who knew the carefully coded language used by journalists in cases like this, would be able to assume that the official view was that this was a tragic case of suicide. It was a small paragraph that could easily have been missed by anyone who might have been interested. But Stansfield had no family to care about his death and no friends to look after his interests. As it happened, the one person who had more reason to be interested in Stansfield than anyone else did miss this piece of interesting and tragic news.

That situation was corrected five days after the paragraph had been published in the *Dunmerrick Herald*.

Ferrybridge Studio was a squat red sandstone Victorian building of two floors. The front of the building was dominated by a large central upper floor-window. There were small decorative towers on either side of the building. These towers disguised the chimneys. At one time, when the building was still known as Ferrybridge

House, it had been split into two households and it retained two large blue front doors. Gemma Dusk and her husband Robert Walker had retained these doors after they bought the property and in a moment of fun they had labelled them 'His' and 'Hers.'

From the common lobby at the front doors, a wide staircase swept up in a large curve to their home on the upper floor, while downstairs Gemma had her art studio in what she rather grandly, but not too seriously, called the west wing. Similarly, Robert had his recording studio in the east wing.

Robert Walker had the appearance of being a bit wild but was a gentle romantic, a poet, a singer, and a maker of tales that delighted his two nieces. He had met Gemma when he was working for a publisher of children's stories. He was editing children's books; Gemma had been commissioned to provide illustrations for a book called *The Children of Wellwood Forest* (1).

Now, five days after Stansfield's death, Gemma was working in her studio. She heard her phone ringing in what she and Robert called the Thinking Room. This was a large central ground floor room where they entertained visitors, or sat in quiet moments of contemplation. It was a great place to relax, to meditate. There was no television in this room and no radio. There was an odd collection of mismatched but comfortable chairs and an eclectic collection of all sorts of items, mostly of wood, metal or stone, all natural materials. Gemma's favourite was a wooden-framed Victorian hour-glass, which she actually used to restrict her breaks in the Thinking Room.

Robert picked up the phone and chatted pleasantly for a few minutes. Gemma was now in the doorway, the light catching her beautiful long black curly hair that flowed elegantly almost to her waist.

"Catriona," Robert announced.

Gemma took the phone, a warm smile on her heart-shaped face, and drifted casually from her studio into the Thinking Room. Her dark brown eyes were sparkling. She had always been close to her sister and they often had long chats on the phone.

They nattered for a moment or two. Gemma knew her sister better than she knew anyone else in the world and she knew instinctively from the subtle tones and inflections in Catriona's voice that she was bursting to tell her something unusually significant. When she did, Gemma was taken by surprise. Stansfield was dead! Richard Graham Mackenzie Stansfield had gone to meet his Maker and give an account of his conduct while alive. When the call was concluded and the news had sunk in, Gemma inched towards the big old-fashioned wooden fireplace, with its pile of logs at the side. She eyed up her own painting above it. It was not full of vibrant colours like many of her later works. It showed frost covered railway lines vanishing into fog. The only colour was in the red lights of the stop signs. The rest of the painting was grey, many shades of cold grey.

A small brass plaque told that *Fogbound* had won the national Brushworks under 18s art prize in 1998. Gemma was still attending Dunmerrick Academy at the time that she had painted it and had only just started studying art. The judges had been impressed by the way Gemma had captured the almost mysterious atmosphere of the misty fog and with her successful use of a variety of shades of grey which made the painting so atmospheric.

But that painting held hidden meanings, dark secret meanings that Gemma had only ever shared with her sister, her parents and with Robert. When she painted the scene, Gemma's mind did not see a fogbound railway scene. In her mind, the railway lines vanishing into the mist represented her future, which at the time she painted it was so uncertain. The red lights represented her life, which was on hold and the shades of frosty grey represented her mood which was slowly emerging from the cold and total darkness.

Robert eyed Gemma silently from across the room with some concern. The phone call from Catriona had clearly had an impact on Gemma.

Gemma's face had a gentle half smile as she turned to face Robert. She announced in a flat emotionless voice: "Stansfield's dead. Seems to have killed himself at Craigmark." Robert did not respond immediately. He did not display any emotion, other than a weak smile rather like Gemma's. He edged forward and hugged Gemma in a gentle, loving way, stroked her beautiful long hair and commented softly, "Well, I hope that's an end to it all."

An hour or so later Catriona arrived, her husband, Fraser and two young girls in tow. Catriona was very like her sister. She was two years older and was just a little shorter than her younger sister, but she shared the same friendly heart-shaped face and the same dark brown eyes. Like Gemma, Catriona had black hair, but unlike Gemma, Catriona's was straight and fell to just over her shoulders. No one could possibly mistake that they were sisters.

In appearance Fraser was almost the opposite of Robert. He managed a sub-post office for a man who had a chain of four of them. He had a round serious, clean-shaven face and light coloured hair. He came across as being rather formal. Even for this impromptu family gathering, Fraser had put on a suit and a tie. Fraser was a highly respected postal historian and was often asked to give a talk to groups interested in that sort of thing. Everyone else in the family tolerated his hobby, but thought that it was boring.

The girls, Wendy, aged eight, and Kay, aged six, were quite unlike each other. Wendy had inherited her dad's fair hair, though in Wendy's case, her hair was long and very bushy. Kay had her mum's dark hair and dark eyes. They were both a bit excited about the unexpected visit to see Uncle Rob and Auntie Gem. They loved their trips to Robert and Gemma's house.

The youngsters shouted a friendly "Hiya" to Gemma and headed for Uncle Robert. "Tell us a story," they implored.

They all went to the Thinking Room, and each chose one of the mismatched armchairs. The girls loved this room. It was always full of interesting things, tucked away in every corner or sitting quietly on just about every inch of shelf space; things that Gemma used for inspiration for her paintings, or Robert used for ideas for his stories. Often the girls would look around and pick something off a shelf at random and Uncle Robert would have to make up a story about it. There were objects like a piece of driftwood that looked like some kind of wild animal and beside that there sat an ancient toy that had to be wound up with a key instead of being run by a battery. Uncle Robert was always ready with a new story, this time, though, he did not invite the girls to pick something from a shelf. He had a new poem ready for them.

"Well," Robert began, "remember when you came here at New Year and it was snowing?"

The girls nodded with large eager eyes that confirmed that they remembered.

"We built a snowman," Kay, remembered eagerly.

"Well this is a poem about our snowman."

Everyone settled down and waited for Robert to recite his new poem.

"Snowflakes drifting in a casual way,
Falling from a darkened sky,
'It's snowing,' happy children say.
Adults go rushing by.

Coming home towards the ground,
Swirling in the breeze,
Landing softly without a sound,
A speck of earth to freeze.

The children ask: 'Will it lie?'
Mum says she doesn't know.
The children watch the flakes and sigh:
'We want a friend of snow.'

The snow is thick. It's cold and wet,
Eyes watch the children play.
They throw it at the friends they've met.
'Let's make a man,' they say.

The man they made had a heart of ice.
His eyes were made of stone.
The children say they think he's nice,
But soon, he'll be alone.

Now the sun is warm and bright.
The snowman melts away.
He's never seen day or night,
Nor felt the warmth of May.

He's getting smaller hour by hour,
And rising to the sky.
The sun exerts His mighty power,
But snowmen never die.

The snowman now is flying high,
In a cloud that's tumbling round.
The cloud is heavy in the sky,
Snow falls to the ground.

Snowflakes drifting in a casual way,
Falling from a darkened sky,
'It's snowing,' happy children say.
Adults go rushing by.

The girls laughed and clapped their hands. Catriona
and Gemma nodded their approval with appreciative
smiles. Then, as the two men and the two children went

upstairs to Robert's Den, Kay could be heard asking. "Can you write a poem about me?"

Catriona had brought a bottle of wine and she and Gemma settled down to celebrate the good news. Stansfield was dead!

Even if they had known in time, neither Gemma nor Catriona would have had any interest in attending Stansfield's funeral. It was good enough to know that Stansfield was dead and gone.

As it happened a briefer than usual ceremony was held at Meadowlands Crematorium and apart from the crematorium staff and The Rev Mark Lucas, from Dunmerrick Parish Church, the only people there were Maria O'Connell from Craigmark Hospital, Inspector Quentin from the police and Mandy Stafford, who sat discretely at the back of the hall in which the service was held. None of those present had any emotional connections to Stansfield. Stansfield had no family and he had no friends to mourn his passing. The staff at the crematorium were simply doing the work that they were paid to do. The Rev Lucas gave a rather automatic, and Mandy thought, insincere service. If he did have any thoughts about Stansfield, the man, he kept them to himself. Maria was there because she felt that it would have been unchristian of her not to be there.

Maria and Inspector Quentin had met briefly during the investigation into Stansfield's death. After the service they exchanged pleasantries in an almost formal way but neither even mentioned the name of the dead man.

The situation was almost as if, with the passing of Richard Graham Mackenzie Stansfield, his memory was already being erased by those who had at some time encountered him.

Mandy Stafford was on the reporting staff at the *Dunmerrick Herald*. She had been there for more years than she cared to think about. She had been there since she was a teenager and she was now on the wrong side of 40. Mandy had shoulder length vivid red hair and she did not need a bag of make up to make herself look exceptionally pretty.

She noted the presence at the funeral service of Inspector Quentin and the Rev Mark Lucas. She knew them having spoken to them before. She would phone them later. The other mourner, she did not know. In the car park after the service, Mandy approached Maria and introduced herself. But Maria told her nothing much, only that she was at the service representing Craigmark Hospital, and when she was asked about Stansfield, Maria became very proper and correct. She told Mandy that she would have to contact the Health Board's public information office.

Mandy had a reputation for being thorough, fair and honest in her reporting. She had wondered about Stansfield. In the general rush in the couple of days before every issue of a weekly newspaper is printed, everything seems to get done in a rush and the paragraph about Stansfield's suicide had slipped into the *Dunmerrick Herald* without embellishment. But with publication, Mandy went to the steel grey metal filing cabinet beside her office desk and made a search. This cabinet was used to store newspaper cuttings. She pulled out Stansfield's file... and began to wonder. Was there, perhaps, a story behind his death?

Mandy phoned Inspector Quentin who was, as she expected, also very proper and repeated only that an investigation was still under way and that in due course a report would go to the procurator fiscal.

The Rev Lucas merely commented that he had talked with Stansfield on a few occasions at Craigmark Hospital and that he appeared to be a rather sad and lonely individual.

There was nothing there for Mandy to make a story. But Mandy was a meticulous and methodical reporter. As well as the filing cabinet of newspaper cuttings that was kept at the office, Mandy kept another filing cabinet at her home in Meadowbrook Place on the Witchcairn estate (2). What secrets lay in this cold steel grey cabinet?

It was in here that Mandy kept all the notes that she had ever made while researching and checking her stories, whether or not the stories had ever been written. It was a habit that started at the very beginning of her career as a journalist and one that provided so much information that was not in the cuttings file, that on many occasions it had proven invaluable for Mandy's work. Her notes were kept in a collection of small mismatched recycled envelopes, mostly in shades of brown, cream and white but also in bright blue, red and even green.

That evening, Mandy took her rather unhelpful notes from the funeral service, and her conversations with those who had been there. She dated and sourced them, and then she opened her own file of notes relating to the late Richard Graham Mackenzie Stansfield to drop in the new ones in when some long forgotten piece of paper came to hand. Here Mandy found a scribbled note of information that had never been made public, and it linked Stansfield with a young Gemma Dusk. Mandy knew Gemma, not well, not as a friend, but over the years she had written several features about Gemma's outstanding work as an artist. Mandy pondered on the link that she had just rediscovered. But there was nothing at all to suggest that after so many years, this link had anything to do with Stansfield's suicide.

It did not take long for the official reports to be made up. Everyone involved concluded that Stansfield had stopped taking his medication, had become depressed and had taken his own life by hanging himself until he was dead.

Staff at the hospital were criticised for failing to ensure that he was taking his medicine, for not noticing that his condition had changed and that he was going into a spiral of depression. Had Stansfield any relatives, one of them might have been inclined to take this matter further. But Stansfield had been alone in the world. Staff felt that some of the criticism in the report was a bit too strong, but systems and checks at the hospital were quickly improved.

CHAPTER THREE:

RICHARD GRAHAM MACKENZIE STANSFIELD

We are not born with goodness or badness. That is something we learn.

- Dr Greta Brentwood, *Mind of a Killer*, 1983.

With the investigation into Stansfield's death completed, the few items that had belonged to him were gathered together and returned to Craigmark Hospital. There was one set of hospital issue clothes, which included a pair of soft slip on shoes - size eight. There was a handful of loose change, one small bar of chocolate, a few toiletries, a good luck medallion, a notebook and a blunt pencil and one ring, apparently made of gold and possibly a wedding ring.

Maria O'Connell was an administrative manager with responsibilities for both Craigmark and Knadger House hospitals. She had been in that post since moving to the area from Stirling three years before. She was also chairman of the Patient Welfare Committee, a group of dedicated volunteers who helped to cater for all sorts of little extras for the patients and their visitors. This voluntary work was once again for both hospitals.

Maria O'Connell was a rather burly woman in her mid fifties. She had a round friendly face and eyes that retained the sparkle of youth. Her hair fell down by the sides of her face and was a shade of what looked like faded red. She managed the faintest hint of a sympathetic smile which hardly showed on her slightly wrinkled face as she eyed up the pathetic little collection of items and sighed.

"It's not much for the whole of a man's life," she sympathised in her soft Cork accent.

Amelia Foxton, a young nursing assistant who was also one of the Welfare Committee volunteers, echoed Maria's thoughts by quoting a line from one of her favourite songs. *"Imagine no possessions. I wonder if you can* (1)."

Maria had, as they say, a heart of gold. In normal circumstances, it would have been up to hospital administration to simply return a deceased patient's belongings to the next of kin, but Stansfield's hospital record listed no next of kin, no relatives, and no friends. There was no one in the world to care about him; no one to mourn his tragic passing. There was no one to claim his few belongings. That is how Maria O'Connell came to be in possession of Stansfield's notebook. Maria was the type of person who only ever saw the good in people. In her eyes a certain light outlined the shadows. She was always the first to defend any of the patients when they did something wrong. She may not have liked all the patients, but she did not dislike any of them. It would have been unchristian to do so and Maria was a good Christian woman. She drew her strength from her religion.

She did not place much significance in Stansfield's notebook, not at first. After all, the police investigating Stansfield's death had carefully studied its contents and they had concluded that it contained nothing more than the incoherent ramblings of a semi-literate and seriously ill and disturbed patient.

She took the notebook home with her on the off-chance that there was a clue about a relative or a friend, or perhaps a clue about why he had decided to kill himself. Suicide, what a terrible sin against The Lord. When she found the time to take a look at the notebook, she settled into her softest armchair with a mug of coffee and picked it up. It was rather like an old school jotter. She flicked through the pages. Only the first dozen or so pages had anything written on them. The rest of the pages had been left blank. All the writing was large and childishly untidy and written in pencil rather than ink.

Maria went to the first page. There was no title, no introduction and no date. She started reading the first entry.

They stole my car and drove it into the lake I know they did cos I seen them do it but the police dint belief me when I told them what I seen. They dint belief that they left me by the lake and they dint belief that someone stole my house

There was a line of space here and Maria read the paragraph again, to try to get a clearer idea of what Stansfield was saying. She closed her eyes. She wondered if Stansfield had stopped here because the effort of writing about this had been too much for him. She sipped on her coffee before returning to Stansfield's epic.

While Maria was checking Stansfield's notebook in her flat on Suspension Avenue, someone else was reading about Stansfield on the other side of town. Mandy Stafford had settled down with a bottle of beer. At the offices of the Dunmerrick Herald, Mandy liked to think of herself as one of the lads and that had given her a taste for beer, and wherever possible, real ales. One of her hobbies was home brewing, but her latest batch of home brew was, well, brewing.

Mandy curled up on her sofa and pulled out a handful of newspaper cuttings and notes about Stansfield. She started piecing together some information about him. His mother was Kathleen Mackenzie who was a full 14 inches shorter than her husband. She worked for Peter Hufton who ran a local corner newsagent's shop in Dunmerrick.

As Richard began to grow up, it was clear that he was not the brightest of children. In his earliest years the young Stansfield quickly learned how to be disruptive, because it was the only way that he could get all the attention he desperately needed.

Maria read on:

I got my foot hurt bad once I dont remember the pain but the fuss I ended up in the hospital but I dont think it has anything to do with being in hospital now

There was another line of space here.

Mandy sifted through the papers that told of a family tragedy that claimed the lives of Stansfield's parents. She crosschecked notes and published articles. Perhaps somewhere in Stansfield's past there was something worth a story.

His father was Richard Stansfield, a man of 6ft 2in, but whose slim build had earned him the nickname of Pencil-man. His rugged appearance was a result of years of working out of doors. He worked for the local parks department, taking great pride in helping to keep flowerbeds in the local parks looking good all the year round, keeping paths clear, the grass at an acceptable level and keeping the weeds at bay. Those who worked with him found him an inspiration.

Maria read on.

Maybe the ghosts done it all I think my house was honted by ghosts cos a lot of funny things kept on happening there they put lights on and taps and they kept messing with the electric stuff like heaters and things and the tins and stuff got taken out the cuboard and frige I think the ghosts done it all to me.

Maria sighed. The only ghost she believed in was the Holy Ghost. She looked across to the wall of her living room to where she had hung portraits of the Holy Father and of Jesus Christ.

When I was at school I got into the football team but we got beat and they all said it was my fault and no one liked me but I dint care

One time me and Butch got a day off school we went to the park and bilt a big snowman we went there a lot cos I remember catching fish in a jar on a sunny day

Maria rubbed her tired eyes. The police were almost certainly right. There was nothing comprehensible in the notebook. And yet, she was sure that Stansfield had wanted to say something, either to himself or to someone else.

Mandy was becoming convinced that there really was no news story in all these cuttings and notes. She knew of the link between Stansfield and Gemma Dusk, but it appeared to be isolated. Now that Stansfield was dead, was there actually a story here? Was there any point in bringing up his past?

Mandy checked cuttings and notes on Gemma Dusk but there was nothing new, just that single unpublished link.

Maria downed more coffee and read on.

There was snow and ice and I was at home waiting for mum and dad and I was watching the tv when the police came to the house and

Maria wondered about that. The other sentences were a bit muddled but this one just stopped as if the memory had been too hard to find or too painful to go over.

When I got home from my holiday the house wasnt there someone had stole it I dint no what to do so I got out the car and thats when it got stole to and then the other car came up and I got in to follow my car

Maria thought that she should have been drinking Irish coffee instead of instant coffee. She turned to the notebook once more. Maria found it increasingly difficult to understand just what Stansfield was trying to say.

When the woman left me at the side of the lake she took my clothes and gave me a big coat with sanwiches in the pocket and some beer and the police dint belief me

Maria swallowed hard and shook her head. She wondered just how much more of this she could endure and decided, not much. She flicked through the pages, just glancing at the untidy scrawl. Then one phrase slapped her hard in the face.

.... I stayed there with my wife and she left me ...

Maria stared at the page and read the paragraph twice more to make sure that she had not made a mistake.

Me and mum and dad was all living in a house near the river and then I stayed there on my own and then I stayed there with my wife and she left me but she was a whore bitch anyway

Maria found herself grasping the cross that she always wore around her neck and quietly saying, "Oh dear God" to herself out of sympathy for the poor tormented soul of the late Richard Graham Mackenzie Stansfield. Kind-hearted Maria knew that even if Stansfield had been married and divorced; yes, even divorced, even if there was nothing to pass on, it was her Christian duty to find his former wife and let her know that Stansfield was dead. Maria decided that in the morning, she would take another look at the hospital records relating to Richard Graham Mackenzie Stansfield.

The ring. Maria suddenly remembered the gold ring. She had wondered about it. Now she was sure that it was a wedding ring. She inspected it. There was an inscription and perhaps a hallmark on the inside, but Maria could not quite make it out. She decided she would have to take it to an expert. There was a shop in town which would be able to help.

Maria wrote a little memo to herself in her pocket diary: *Check records, check ring; speak to Rev Lucas, call David.*

Next day at the hospital, Maria checked over the files on Stansfield. There was not much in the record, other than medical notes of what medication he had been given, but Maria did piece together some of the basics from additional notes attached to Stansfield's files. Maria started putting together something of Stansfield's muddled life.

In summary, Richard Graham Mackenzie Stansfield was born at Knadger House Hospital on the evening of April 23, 1980.

It was not a particularly difficult birth, but the length of time his mum, Kathleen was in labour caused some concern.

Kathleen insisted that he be named Richard, after his father and paternal grandfather, Graham, after her father, and Mackenzie so he would always be linked to her family name. Four names, she insisted, was enough for anyone.

Stanfield's last address was listed as Glenbank Cottage and it had a hand written note beside the entry reading, 'Now demolished.'

There was no mention of any relative, no mention of a wife or ex-partner. Thinking about Stansfield, Maria could not remember Stansfield ever having had a visitor, other than The Rev Mark Lucas, the hospital chaplain.

Maria knew that if anyone would be able to help solve the mystery of Stansfield's missing wife, it would be David Yorke. She decided in the morning she would phone him to arrange to meet him.

Maria had stopped reading the notebook at the mention by Stansfield of 'my wife.' She was now determined to find her. If Maria had read the rest of Stansfield's notes she would have found the reference to Bowhouse. If she had found that, she would have understood a lot more about Richard Graham Mackenzie Stansfield.

Mandy Stafford knew all about Bowhouse and, having refreshed her mind, she knew more about Stansfield than Maria ever suspected. If Maria had read

Mandy's file on Stansfield she would have known exactly what he had meant when he wrote: *Bowhouse My fault*

Maria and Mandy were not the only people who had taken an interest in Richard Graham Mackenzie Stansfield. Some years before all this, Gemma Dusk had wheedled Stansfield's school report out of a reluctant school secretary and had logged the details in her own filing system.

At the end of his first year at Wellington Street Primary School a meeting of those concerned decided that although he appeared to be a slow learner, he was not so slow that he should go to a special school. He was a borderline case.

In retrospect that about summed up many of the major decisions in Stansfield's life. He was a borderline case and meetings of people who did not know him took decisions that would affect the rest of his life.

In the case of the rather slow learner they decided to have him stay in Primary 1 for another year and join the new intake of infants.

In this second go at a Primary 1 class Stansfield met the one person he could describe as a friend.

He was Ben McCutcheon, who within a couple of years was the school bully. This friendship may have seemed a little odd because bullies usually pick their friends because they have a bit of muscle. They pick them for their own protection. That was not the case in this instance and it was McCutcheon, known to everyone as Butch, who took it upon himself to protect the weaker Stansfield.

For Stansfield, this had the advantage that he was not teased at school as much as he might have been and he was never seriously bullied. But it had the disadvantage that Butch often led Stansfield astray. And while Butch knew the difference between right and wrong, Stansfield did not

CHAPTER FOUR:

QUESTIONS, QUESTIONS, MORE QUESTIONS

Whomsoever does not dare to question will surely learn nothing.

- Isaac Noble Harrington, The Nature of Nature, 1721.

Questions, questions. Everyone seemed to have questions about Richard Graham Mackenzie Stansfield.

The police had been asking questions about him. They had to be satisfied that his death was what it appeared to be, a tragic case of suicide. The hospital managers had been asking questions too, though they were more concerned about hospital routines and how it was that a patient had managed to kill himself, assuming, of course, that it was suicide.

And Maria O'Connell was asking questions. She was trying to find out if there was anyone Stansfield's belongings could be passed on to.

The Drunken Sailor with its reputation for good food and good service was always a favourite place for Maria to eat out. She loved the collection of photographs of old Dunmerrick, antique advertising posters and various artefacts that adorned the walls and hung from the ceiling.

Maria sat alone at a table for two in the lounge with a clutter of papers around her. She was reading intently, taking notes of interesting details as she came across them, only occasionally lifting her eyes to squint around the room.

She failed to notice the man approaching the table until a fake Irish accent asked: "Now what would the queen o' Cork be doing in an English pub like this?"

Maria hardly looked up, but gently scolded the visitor. "Now, what would the Irish be wanting with queen at all, and have ye forgotten already, that you now live in Scotland, not England?"

The new arrival was David Yorke, a tall thin man who had sprouted a tightly cropped beard and moustache, and had equally short but equally ginger hair.

They looked at each other and broad smiles broke out on their faces. They hugged and gave each other a friendly gentle kiss on the cheek.

"Ah, Maria O'Connell, If only I had met you first..."

"Stop it, David. How is Margaret? The kids?"

"All fine. Judy starts university after the summer."

"Judy? No. Last time I saw her, she was only this high."

"Time flies."

They discussed the menu and placed their orders. David eyed Maria wondering what this meeting was about. Not just lunch, that was sure. Maria didn't work that way.

"So, Maria, me dear, what is it this time? There never was a time that you asked me to lunch that there wasn't a favour to be asked." The fake Irish accent was back.

"And there never was a favour asked of you that you didn't do willingly."

David was an expert in ancestry research. He did quite a bit of work for clients and at one time had toyed with the idea of setting up his own business.

Maria explained about the death of Richard Graham McKenzie Stansfield. How he had no friends, no relatives, except, perhaps, a divorced wife. She gave him some notes with details of Stansfield's last address, and some other information gleaned from the medical records and from his notebook.

Over lunch Maria summed up what she knew about Stansfield:

"At the age 21, in 1997, he was admitted to A&E with severe injuries to the head, eyes, face, shoulder, wrist and genitals. Someone must have given him a good going over. At that time his address was at Riverside Terrace. There's a bit of a gap – almost ten years. Then he turned up as a patient at Craigmark in 2007. When he was admitted, the address was Glenbank Cottage but the forms have no next of kin at all, and no friends. As far as I know, the only visitor he ever got was the hospital chaplain.

"But among his possessions there is a ring, a wedding ring, I think. I need to have it checked."

David asked some questions, but for many of them, Maria had no answer and simply shrugged. She was heartened when David told her that finding a marriage certificate would be easy. They arranged to meet again a week later in the Horseshoe Café.

The centre of Dunmerrick was dominated by an ancient volcanic plug; a hill which rose sharply out of the otherwise rather flat landscape. On top of the hill there was a castle. Some historians claimed that the earliest parts of this castle pre-dated the Christian era by two thousand years. Not much was done with the ruin until the 1970s when it was restored, made safe and opened to the public. The broken fragments of road around the base of the hill were joined together to form a ring road, which the civic fathers of the day decided to name Castle Circus. In light of local protests, some parts of this ring road also retained their old names such as Castle Hill Road, Castlehill Gate and The Vennel. Opening the castle to the public brought in tourists and with them came a few souvenir shops and teashops.

One such place was The Horseshoe. It took its name from its architecture. The red sandstone building had once been a warehouse for grain, but the part that was now a café seemed to have been the entrance to the courtyard and stables. The café's front door and windows were quite small, but were surrounded by stonework in the unmistakable shape of a horseshoe.

This establishment had the reputation of having a selection of fine teas and coffees, as well as some of the best cupcakes and scones in the area. The café was a favourite haunt of young people, but they welcomed everyone and it was not just a young crowd who went there. The floor was of bare polished wood, like a church hall, and there were only a dozen tables, each with four chairs. It was rather quaint.

David checked the menu and chose the house speciality: A coffee with the additional flavour of roasted hazelnuts and sweetened, if required, by a light and locally produced honey.

Maria arrived ten minutes late – not like her at all. She was puffing slightly. "Sorry, I was doing a bit of shopping."

They ordered: house speciality for David, without the sweetener, and black tea with lemon for Maria and two cupcakes.

Then it was down to business.

"To get right to the point," David mused, "this Stansfield chap was not married, at least he did not get married in Scotland and I can narrow down that ten year gap.

"His parents were Richard and Kathleen. I found death certificates for them. They were killed in a car crash in January, 1997. The family home was at Riverside Terrace. Now, that was a council house at the time and Richard was allowed to stay on his own as the new tenant."

"Yes," Maria replied. "I think he might have said something like that in his notebook." She fumbled among her papers, found what she was looking for and read from a page of her notes. 'Me and mum and dad was all living in a house near the river and then I stayed there on my own but then I stayed there with my wife...' David, could he have got married on holiday?"

"Then, I ran a search on that Glenbank Cottage. It was out near Loch Marr, opposite Poets' Tryst. Do you know it?"

"I know Poets' Tryst, yes."

"Anyway, I went out there. I don't think the cottage is there any more."

In his brief pause, Maria confirmed his belief.

"I have a note saying Glenbank was demolished."

David went on, "I did find a death certificate for Rose Blair Mackenzie... aged 97. She died in January, 2006. Her address at that time was Glenbank Cottage and your Stansfield chap was living there at that time.

"Well, she wasn't his wife."

"A great aunt is my guess. I don't think he was ever married. There's no record of a marriage and no record of a divorce.

"But the notebook said, 'When my wife left me...'

"A girlfriend maybe. It may have been a short-term relationship. Maybe it seemed like a proper marriage to him. The ring? What about the ring?"

"I've not had a chance to check it out. I was going to take it to McConkey's, but I forgot to bring it with me today."

"So, it's a bit of a dead end. What will you do?"

"What I always do, David." She fingered the cross that was on a chain round her neck. "I'll put my faith in the Lord Jesus Christ. He'll guide me."

David reached for his wallet. Maria stopped him telling him that he had been generous enough already.

"Well, I really have to fly, but, you know, keep in touch. Don't wait till you have another favour to ask. He leaned over and again kissed Maria gently on the cheek, leaving her to settle the bill. Outside the cafe a pair of students glided by handing out leaflets. David took one and casually glanced at it.

It was advertising a one-woman art exhibition. That woman was Gemma Dusk, the local girl who was something of a celebrity in the art world.

In the centre of the front of the leaflet there was a picture of one of the artist's works. David stared at it for moment. The caption beneath it read: Glenbank Cottage, March, 2007.

Maria's words of a moment ago echoed in his mind: "I'll put my faith in the Lord Jesus Christ. He'll guide me."

He went back in to the Horseshoe Cafe and almost collided with Maria making her way out. He showed her the leaflet and pointed out the illustration.

"Well," Maria said softly. "It looks like I've not reached a dead end after all. I think I'll have to visit an art show and speak to this Gemma Dusk."

Before the day of Gemma's exhibition in the John Curdie Gallery, Maria made a point of speaking to The Rev Lucas but did not learn anything new about Stansfield. The Rev Lucas told her that he thought that Stansfield was a pleasant but rather sad and lonely soul. However, he was fairly sure that he remembered Stansfield, once, and only once, refer to his wife, saying that she had beautiful long black hair.

The uncertainty aside, this statement disturbed Maria but by now she had almost convinced herself that Stansfield had never been married.

The questions asked by the police team investigating the death of Stansfield had apparently been answered beyond any reasonable doubt.

The questions that had been raised by hospital managers and the answers they found were, for the time being, kept in confidential files.

Mandy Stafford had no more questions about Stansfield. Mandy knew as much as she needed to know about Richard Graham Mackenzie Stansfield and she thought she knew as much as she needed to know about Gemma Dusk. That link, that isolated single link between Richard Graham Mackenzie Stansfield and Gemma Dusk, no longer seemed to be important. Mandy was sure of it.

As far as Gemma Dusk was concerned, she no longer had any questions about Stansfield. At one time he did have, but all her questions had been answered a long time ago.

CHAPTER FIVE:

GEMMA DUSK

Whatever talents young people have should be encouraged.

Fergus Overman, *Education in Modern Times*, 1973.

Maria O'Connell stood in Market Square, looking at the magnificent building which housed the John Curdie Art Gallery (1). It had once been the offices of Dunmerrick Burgh Council. Construction had just been completed when Germany invaded Poland, the Second World War started and the building was immediately commandeered by the military as a warehouse for uniforms. It was an imposing structure which dominated the square as much now as it had in 1939. She scanned the building. The front of the structure had a substantial rotunda with a green copper dome. The base of the building had shining black marble and the rest of it consisted of substantial blocks of blonde Portland stone. Maria thought it gave the impression of being substantial and solid, like a bank. The high windows on the ground floor made the place an ideal venue for an art gallery when the Burgh Council was replaced by remote district and regional councils.

Maria looked at the leaflet promoting the new exhibition by Gemma Dusk. Invited guests were to arrive at 12.30 for 1pm, when there would be an official opening ceremony, with a talk about some of the paintings by the artist herself. The exhibition would be open to the public from 2pm. Maria checked her watch. It was only 12.10. She had plenty of time for other business first.

Maria had been meaning to take a trip into town so she could take Stansfield's gold ring into McConkey's shop in Victoria Street. But she had been busy with other things and on the days that she had been in town, she had forgotten to take the ring with her.

Victoria Street fed into the Market Square. It ran directly off the square, almost on a north-south line. It was only a couple of minutes walk to the shop she wanted to visit. Victoria Street was the town's main commercial street and most of the buildings were imposing and impressive. Many of them had been built in opulent

Victorian times when money, it seemed, was not too much of a problem, not for constructing impressive buildings anyway.

Like several other shops in this area, McConkey's clock and jeweller's shop was a long established family business. The shop was on the ground floor of a three storey building. The windows were brightly lit and displayed a variety of watches, rings and other precious items.

The door opened smoothly and silently, apart from the tinkle of a very small bell and as soon as Maria closed the door, the noise of the outside world seemed to be shut out.

The new sound inside the shop was that of dozens of clocks.

The shop gave the immediate impression of somewhere you should not speak too loudly; somewhere you should treat with the utmost respect, like a cathedral or a graveyard. Everything was bright and clean, almost too clean,

A pretty young woman with curly black hair and a friendly smile emerged from somewhere and asked if she could help. She was casually dressed in jeans and a red sweatshirt with the slogan, "I've got time on my hands."

Maria explained that she had a ring but could not read the inscription on the inside of it.

"Not to worry", said the friendly girl. She took the ring and looked at the inside of it closely through a magnifying glass.

"Ah, yes. I see it. It's a bit faded. Not to worry." She placed the ring on a device that looked a bit like a microscope. An image of the inside of the ring flashed up a television screen above the device. The girl twiddled a knob and the image sharpened to reveal the secrets of the ring. The letters KM and RS were faint but clear and there was a heart between them. Looking at the hallmark, the girl told Maria that the ring had been made in England in 1978. It dawned on Maria at once that this was not Stanfield's own ring. It was his father's. She had not even considered that as a possibility. She had been too focused on the idea that this was Stansfield's own wedding ring. It had all been a lot easier and a lot quicker than Maria had anticipated.

As she left McConkey's she automatically peered in the window of the shop next door, Principal Lighting. This was a lighting shop run by Stevie Prince. His teenage son, Innes was in the window, changing the display. The shop sold all manner of lamps and lights, free standing, wall-mounted, ceiling mounted, indoor lights, outdoor lights, fun lamps, security lights, lights, in fact, for every occasion. The talking point in Dunmerrick was frequently the window display which always had something odd in it. Everyone in Dunmerrick looked in the window of this shop. Everyone talked about it. On display this time there was a bath with the side cut out of it to allow its conversion to a sofa. There was a bird cage suspended from the ceiling, but with a fish tank inside it. Light bulbs suspended from the ceiling gave the impression that they were falling like raindrops and this was heightened by umbrellas painted in the backdrop.

Innes was working at the blackboard. It had the shop slogan printed on it in bold white capital Letters: FUN NEEDS LIGHT and it had a spotlight on the chalked message which Innes changed once or twice a week. He wiped out, 'Open seven days – except Sunday', and added, 'Bargain basement upstairs.'

Maria smiled, thinking about the bath-chair, and headed back to the Curdie Gallery. She did not have an invitation to the opening event, but when she went into the building, she was not asked to produce one.

In the reception area a full size knitted version of Gemma Dusk silently greeted visitors. Behind her there was a prominent sign demanding: *Please switch off your mobile phone* and below it another saying, *No photography*. Immediately next to these signs there was a wall-mounted frame, like a cabinet. On the top of the frame there was a decorative pine board with the word *Trophies* presented in bold gold lettering. The frame that looked like a cabinet had about a dozen cameras and phones apparently nailed to the wall. Maria quickly fumbled in her bag for her phone and switched it off.

She scanned the information board which announced events and gave directions to three exhibitions. The Main Gallery had an exhibition of the work of Charles Rennie Macintosh, Gallery Two had an exhibition called Weather and the Round Room had

Germma's exhibition.

Maria picked up a brochure which outlined the new exhibition and gave some of Gemma's background. On the front of the brochure there was Gemma's painting of the Houses of Parliament, dated 2010. It was clearly one of her newest works.

The Curdie Gallery was more than just an art gallery. Apart from the three large rooms equipped to display artworks, there was a hall for concerts and performing arts.

There was also a shop, with various books and souvenirs and this was set around the reception desk. Maria noticed a selection of postcards with Gemma's work on them. Maria hesitated, wondering if she should go to the Gallery's McMillan Café (2). It would give her time to read more about Gemma and her work, but on reflection she thought she knew a fair bit about Gemma, after all the Dunmerrick Herald frequently wrote about her and her art.

Feeling rather nervous about gatecrashing, Maria entered the Round Room and was relieved to see a familiar figure in the form of Frank Hastings. Frank was a neighbour from Suspension Avenue and one of the friendliest and most genuine people Maria had come across. They knew each other well. Maria should have realised that Frank would have been here. He was an art teacher at Dunmerrick Academy and was involved in the local arts group. She would get a word with him when he was not so busy. Looking at him Maria had the impression that he was in charge of the event.

Maria looked around the room. It was fairly busy. Some people had dressed formally for the occasions while others were in casual dress. Most people stood around in groups of two, three or four, chatting. Maria became aware of the noise from the people. It was like the buzzing of bees in a beehive. She also became aware that most people were holding a paper plate with finger snacks, or a glass of white wine.

She made her way to the table to get some for herself. Then she started slowly exploring Gemma's work. Looking round Maria could see just why Gemma's paintings had become so popular. Some of the works on display were paintings of flowers in vibrant colours. She recognised views of the local Hudson Park and the Hay Park, painting in beautiful spring or autumn colours.

She had not made much progress on her way around the Round Room when the gathering was called to order by Frank Hastings.

"Ladies and gentlemen," he called loudly, and as the general noise and clatter faded away, he lowered his own voice. Mandy Stafford started taking some notes.

"I am Frank Hastings, your... eh ... master of ceremonies for today. As chairman of the Dunmerrick Arts Group it is my very great pleasure to welcome you all here today and to call on two exceptional ladies.... Gemma, of course, who will speak to you in a few moments about some of her work, but here to introduce her and to officially open the exhibition, I ask you to welcome our local MSP, Samantha Bertellotti."

Ms Bertellotti was given a resounding welcome. She was clearly a popular politician. She spoke about how pleased she was with the latest improvements to the building and she added a little piece of news that few in the room were aware of.

"As I am sure, you all know, our parliament building in Edinburgh has a lot of space for the display of public arts and I am very pleased to say that earlier this week, one of the new works placed there is a piece by Gemma."

She turned to Gemma. "Gemma's work in the parliament building is her painting of the Spirit of Scotland Sculpture at Loudoun Hill and I am sure you know that this represents matters from our history that are close to my heart" (3).

She spoke for just a few moments more before she officially declared the exhibition open. Then she called Gemma to the platform to speak about her work.

Gemma being a very informal person, was always a bit uncertain about what to wear at events such as this. She had chosen a deep purple dress with a few pretty frills artistically placed from the waist down. Gemma's long black hair seemed to sparkle, like her, and it shimmered as she moved. She looked elegant and many eyes followed her as she took her place.

"Thank you for that. As most of you know I now live on the east coast, but I am absolutely thrilled to be back in Dunmerrick: Mostly because I get free bed and breakfast here. Thanks, mum."

The audience laughed and Maria could see that Gemma was not at all nervous. She was genuinely happy and totally relaxed talking to the crowd and she told a little of her early days in Dunmerrick.

Then it came to the thanks. "I want to thank my parents for constant encouragement and my sister, Catriona, who has been a pillar for me all my life, and my ever-patient husband, Robert." As she mentioned each name she nodded to them and they in turn acknowledged the thanks with a nod or a brief wave.

Maria thought it all sounded like a film awards ceremony.

"There are a few people here I want to thank. Mr Hastings here was my art teacher at Dunmerrick Academy. When I took his classes he was very supportive and always encouraged me to explore my own techniques and my own ideas and he gave me the best advice on how to get the very best results. Thank you, Mr Hastings.

In fact, one of the first works of art that I produced while I was still at school was *Fogbound*. It won an award and I still cherish the award and the painting. Actually, that painting is on display in this exhibition.

"Of course, *Fogbound* was not my very first painting. I expect most of you have heard the story… the story that I have often dismissed. Every now and then it crops up in newspapers or magazines. It says something like this. When I was four, I was messing about with some paints. There was a sports event on the TV and I painted an apparently superb – well, for a four-year old – painting of a javelin thrower. Mum was so impressed by it she kept it. Not long after that I am supposed to have painted an impressive image of a ballet dancer and again mum was sufficiently impressed to keep the painting.

"In fact, the truth is just a bit less interesting. Both paintings are just random splashes and lines, just a bit of fun, and the fact is that no one in the family can now be certain if they were my paintings or Catriona's.

"Somehow these two items have found their way into this exhibition, despite the fact they were not on the list that I approved. Thanks, mum," she added with a smile.

"Well, I can live with the story. A journalist friend once told me, 'When the legend is more interesting than the truth, print the legend.'

"I have just returned from a few weeks in London and I took the opportunity of painting a couple of well known London landmarks. Those works are here too, so this exhibition covers some of my very earliest and some of my most recent works. I hope you enjoy them. Thank you."

Soon everyone was able to mingle again. Maria hesitantly introduced herself to Gemma. Maria was a good judge of facial language and could tell that Gemma was happy to meet her.

"I wondered," Maria hesitated, "If you ever knew the people who lived in Glenbank Cottage."

"Not really. No."

"You see the man who lived there, Richard Stansfield... he died recently, and I have a few things that belonged to him."

It was just a flash in Gemma's eyes, but Maria had spotted it.

"I didn't really know him. Our paths crossed. That's all."

"Oh, well it's just that I have his notebook and things."

Gemma blanched. "Notebook?" she asked weakly.

"Yes. He mentioned his wife in it."

"Wife?" Gemma's surprise was genuine and taking her cue from Maria's look of curiosity she added. "I didn't know he had a wife. I don't think he was ever close to anyone."

"But you hardly knew him. Your paths just crossed."

Gemma gave a non-committal noise.

"Yes," she confirmed, "our paths just crossed, once, that's all."

She had nothing else to say and Maria knew this was neither the right time nor the right place to press the point. In any case Mandy Stafford from the *Dunmerrick Herald* was waiting patiently to speak to Gemma.

"Well, if you remember anything…. Here, take this." Maria scribbled her phone number on a piece of paper, handed it to Gemma.

Gemma took the piece of paper looking thoughtful. She smiled and gave a gentle but silent nod of her head.

"I might," she commented cautiously and cryptically added, "I need to talk to my sister first."

Mandy took her turn to interview Gemma but had no reason to mention the late Richard Graham Mackenzie

Stansfield, and, of course, she had no idea that Maria O'Connell had just spoken to Gemma about him.

When she returned to the office she wrote up a feature about Gemma's work and the new exhibition. With a selection of pictures it might make a nice two page spread. Back home, Mandy picked up the exhibition brochure, and the promotional leaflet and filed them away with her notes from the day's event.

She settled on the sofa with a bottle of beer, switched on the TV and began to relax. Quite suddenly something in what she had read earlier surfaced in her mind.

She went back to the Gemma Dusk file and there it was. The front of the leaflet had a painting by Gemma of Glenbank Cottage. There was something odd about that cottage. Was it something that had happened there? No, Mandy was sure it had something to do with the building. On a first search of her notes file Mandy found nothing about Glenbank, and yet there was something hidden in her mind about that cottage. What was it? She could not quite remember. Her filing system rarely failed her and just because she had nothing filed under Glenbank Cottage did not mean that there was no note in there, somewhere. Mandy wrote a little note on her To Do list, reminding her to make a more thorough search of the files. She had to find out more about Glenbank Cottage.

CHAPTER SIX:

GEMMA'S STORY

No one ever visits Hell by choice.

Norman Miller, *Collected Adages*, 1991.

The house at number fourteen Headriggs Farm Road was of early 1970s architecture, with an attached garage, a small neat front garden and a larger garden to the rear. Between the front gardens of fourteen and twelve there was a low brick wall and between fourteen and sixteen there was a low and neatly kept privet hedge. Long before the events that changed so many lives, this was the home of the Dusk family.

Alexander and Samantha Dusk bought the house in 1977. In 1980 their first daughter, Catriona was born and she was followed in 1982 by Gemma.

As the girls grew up they were told wonderful tales of their great grandfather. Alexander Dusek was a hero. He was born and brought up in Prague and he was just 23 years old when Germany invaded his country. He escaped. He made his way to Scotland where joined the RAF and fought Nazis throughout the Second World War. Somewhere in the family's time in Scotland the name evolved from Dusek to Dusk.

The younger Alexander Dusk, Catriona and Gemma's father, was an engineer with a long established local company that was now just a branch office of a large international group. He often worked late shifts, but he earned good money. His only hobby, and the family tended to find this rather odd, was collecting coffee mugs that advertised chocolate. He had a great time every Easter , searching for new promotional items.

Samantha was a supervisor at a large out of town supermarket, where her hours rarely matched requirements. She also volunteered one day a week in the local hospice shop.

The girls were not identical of course, but they looked so much alike that no one would ever question that they were sisters.

Catriona loved to read. She read everything and she had a mind that was quick and sharp. She could quickly spot flaws in any story. Gemma loved swimming and athletics. On the field and in the pool she was fast and she was strong. She often represented her school at national events.

The girls had always been close, secretive even. Now that special bond was more important than ever.

In the days that followed her exhibition in the John Curdie Gallery, Gemma spent hours with Catriona discussing the prospect of a further meeting with Maria O'Connell.

Sometimes Gemma warmed to the idea and Catriona was cautious and at other times, these roles were reversed, with Gemma full of doubt and Catriona pushing for a further meeting. Eventually, the girls decided that they had fully exhausted all the possibilities and that their discussions were becoming too repetitive to be worthwhile. More than anything else Gemma worried about what secrets might be hidden in Stansfield's notebook. Catriona agreed that this was something they could not ignore. In the end they took a momentous decision. They would meet Maria together but they had not yet decided if they should tell Maria only what she needed to know, or if they should tell her everything.

It was Catriona who phoned Maria and arranged to meet, as it turned out, in Maria's home. Thinking about it later, Catriona felt that her call had probably been a bit too formal and it might have left Maria a little puzzled.

They arrived in Suspension Avenue where Maria had her flat. The late Victorian red sandstone tenement blocks here had no front gardens, but they did have mature trees in the street outside the houses. Only one side of Suspension Avenue had buildings. The other side was open ground with neatly cut grass in the care of the parks department of the local council.

The street sloped gently down to a suspension footbridge which crossed the River Merrick and went into Hudson Park (1).

Catriona cast an eye over the buildings and, as she had a habit of doing, quickly spotted an oddity. Although the houses were only on one side of the street, they were only given odd numbers, as if when the numbers were allocated, there was a tentative plan to build on the other side. She thought it curious and turned it over in her mind, but she quickly decided that this was not the best time to discuss it with Gemma.

Gemma and Catriona were quite nervous; Maria was curious, but not so curious that she had a notebook and pen beside her. That was a good sign, Catriona thought to herself. When the three ladies had settled down and each had a glass of red wine, Gemma spoke a little hesitantly.

"I'm not quite sure where to begin..."

In her mind, it was, where's the notebook, what's in it? But she did not want to draw attention to Stansfield's notes or her keen interest in the notebook.

In the moment that she paused, Maria urged, "Just start at the beginning."

"Eh, well..."

"Gemma was born at a very early age..."

Maria smiled patiently, but Gemma threw her sister a look of disapproval. She was getting more anxious by the minute.

"When I was at school, primary school, I was quite athletic. I loved running and swimming."

Catriona refrained from saying. 'But not at the same time.' In the hour or so that followed, Gemma told her story and when her emotions started to make Gemma falter, it was Catriona who came in with the help. She knew as much of the tale they were telling as Gemma.

They started hesitantly but soon gained momentum. Maria listened carefully as the story unfolded.

Gemma was a strong swimmer. As a pupil at Wellington Street Primary School and in her earliest years at Dunmerrick Academy, she was in the school swimming team and on several occasions had represented the school at events across Scotland regularly winning medals. On the track she was a fast runner, but her real passion was concentrated on her efforts in the swimming pool. She trained often and the school had an arrangement with the council's leisure department for training young swimmers when the pool was not busy.

One day, during the summer holidays when Gemma was between primary school and Dunmerrick Academy she visited Mastermans collectables shop in Welbeck Street with Catriona. Every inch of wall space was covered with shelves packed with all sorts of strange and wonderful things; toys that had not been played with for many years; advertising signs for products that were no longer sold; pictures, posters, military medals, coins, trinkets and tokens. Gemma could not exactly explain why she had taken Catriona in there... perhaps it was just the fact that the shop window was always so full of odd items. Catriona had taken a liking to a mechanical money bank that had monkeys scampering up and down a tree when a coin was dropped into it. The toy only worked with old pre-decimal pennies, which were also on sale in the shop. Gemma was looking round the displays when she spotted a girl with long red hair. She was a few years older than Gemma (2).

She recognised the red-haired girl from school but could not quite remember her name. The girl picked something out of a box, but gave a sharp scream and dropped it immediately. Gemma thought she must have pricked her finger on the pin of a badge. Catriona had heard the scream and turned in time to see something shiny hit the wooden boarded floor with a dull clatter. She bent down to pick it. The object was a medal with a long neck chain

"There's something wrong with that," the red headed girl said, with a tinge of fear in her voice.

"What is it?" Catriona asked, turning it over to examine it.

"It's a swimming medal," the girl said and added, "But... " then she paused, and gave a gentle shake of her head, before turning and leaving the shop.

"Swimming?" Gemma asked her sister. "Can I see it?"

She took it and looked at both sides of the coin-like medal. On one side it had an engraving of St Andrew and a St Andrew's cross in the background. The other side was plain but was engraved: *Presented to William Kennedy, August 19, 1874* (3).

"There's nothing about swimming on it." Gemma commented.

Catriona looked at it again. "I don't think there's anything wrong with it. I think it is full of good luck."

There was something quite endearing about the medallion and Gemma bought it. As it turned out, she wore it every day... until one day almost four years later the chain broke and Gemma left it at home intending to repair it that evening. That was the day that Gemma's whole world was turned upside down.

She left the medallion beside the mirror on her bedroom table and went out to meet friends, as she often did on Saturday afternoons. She had told her parents that she was going into town but that she would be home in time for tea. However, something happened and she did not come home on this warm and sunny day. Later she could not quite remember exactly what happened. She had been thinking about some of the boys at school. Andy was a bit pompous and a bit arrogant. Stuart was gentle and kind, Murray was still a bit childish. She was turning it all over in her mind, arrogant Andy, moronic Murray and sweet Stuart… There was a van parked partly on the pavement. As she squeezed passed, someone on the inside slid the door open. There was a struggle. Then nothing.

Gemma woke with a start and it took a moment for her to shake off the sleep, but in a long moment she woke, her mind cleared and she started taking in her situation. It terrified her.

She was on a bed, but her movement in the room was restricted by a long chain attached to a wide wrist band on her left arm. The only light in the room came from a single naked bulb. Naked! She was naked.

She quickly discovered that the chain allowed her some movement in the room, but not much. She could reach an improvised toilet, and a basin of cold water, but that was about all. There was a window, but closed curtains of a heavy maroon material covered it. She could not reach the window anyway.

A perfectly rational fear swept through her and even though she knew that the chain would hold her, she made every possible effort to release herself. She succeeded only in making herself tired, sore and angry.

She started screaming, asking if anyone could hear her.

At last a young man appeared at the door of the room. He was wearing a dressing gown. He was quite short, not fat but certainly not skinny. His face was square and a bit flat.

It was strangely pleasant but not what anyone would describe as handsome.

"You're awake. I'm going for a quick shower. I'll be back in a few moments."

His tone was flat and falsely pleasant, and the implication had Gemma even more terrified. She didn't know how long it was before he was back in the room. It was almost certainly less than ten minutes, but it seemed like an eternity. He dropped his dressing gown on to the floor and climbed idly into bed with her. Without a word he slid his body over her.

"Please," Gemma sobbed.

But he wasn't listening. Instead he heaped praise on her, praise that was all the more sickening because of that misleadingly pleasant voice and the fresh after-shower smell.

"Please," Gemma wept again, "I'm only fourteen."

The man stopped. "Liar," he spat angrily. "You're nearly sixteen."

God, how does he know that?

"That's not true," Gemma lied.

97

"Of course it is, Gemma. I know all about you. I know everything about you. I've read all about you. I've seen you swimming."

With that he raped her. Just before he left the room, he turned and casually told Gemma, "I think I'll go and watch a film." He left Gemma lying there, she turned and sobbed into the pillow, wondering if this man had been stalking her for days, weeks, months, perhaps. Or had he just seen a few snippets on the sports pages of the *Dunmerrick Herald*?

At number 14 Headriggs Farm Road, Gemma's mum, her dad and Catriona were frantically phoning everyone they could think of, but no one they called had any idea where Gemma was. Before long, dad phoned the police. While sympathetic, they told him that teenage girls often lost track of time and it was too early for them to file a missing person report.

In her solitude, Gemma thought of home. She thought of her parents and of her sister, Catriona.

Quite suddenly a crazy idea came to her. Maybe she could get in touch with Catriona by telepathy, after all it had happened once before, just once, maybe.

Catriona remembered the excitement in her mother's voice as she told them the story. Catriona had been downstairs, drawing or some such thing. She was quietly singing to herself. It wasn't a song of the day. Catriona's mum recognised it as the Sisters song from the classic film, *White Christmas*.

She thought nothing of it. She was on her way upstairs to remind Gemma to bring down clothes for the wash. Gemma was listening to the radio on headphones. As she turned to see her mum at the bedroom door the plug jumped out of the radio... and yes, Sisters was playing on the radio (4).

The girls tried many times after that to send each other telepathic messages, but it had never worked.

But if ever there was a time for telepathy with Catriona to work, it was now. Gemma tried hard but nothing happened and soon she drifted into an uncomfortable and dreamless sleep.

In the frightening times that she was awake her fears started to overwhelm her. She was certain that she would be killed and perhaps her body would be chopped up and dumped in some remote place. She tried desperately to suppress those fears. She tried to make plans to escape. None of them seemed remotely feasible. She simply could not think properly. Her first thought was to wrap the chain round the man's neck and choke him to death, but she quickly realised that she did not know where the key to the chain lock was. No matter how satisfying it would be to get revenge, this was not a good idea. She needed a better plan.

She was woken from her half sleep state when the man returned, this time fully clothed.

"You must be hungry." That's all he said, and he laid a tray beside her.

She looked at the meal: a beef burger in a bun that had no character and skinny chips. No vegetables, no sauce, no relish. It looked bland and tasteless and it sat on a paper party plate. The fizzy drink beside the burger was in a paper cup. Her meal looked warm rather than hot, but Gemma was hungry enough to eat it. There was no knife and no fork. 'Pity,' she thought to herself contemplating a knife. 'I could have stabbed him.' But then she remembered that she needed him as long as she was chained up and he had the key to the lock.

Gemma let her mind wander back to Catriona. She remembered that as children they used to visit Dunmerrick Castle and play games using not much more than their imagination. They played games about dungeons, dragons and especially about the rescue of Rapunzle with her beautiful long hair. She wished that she could use her beautiful long hair to escape from the prison that she was in.

Gemma drifted once again into an uncomfortable and much broken sleep. In the times that she was awake, Gemma found herself wondering why she kept drifting to sleep. She wondered if the man had drugged her, but there was nothing she could do about it if he had. She started thinking of home and of mum and dad and especially of Catriona. Mum and dad were always there for her, always supportive, always encouraging the girls to develop their imaginations. She thought of happy times like birthdays, Christmas and her dad's habit of springing surprise trips on the girls, like a weekend in York or Aviemore. Mum and dad were always there for them… except this one time. Why were they not here for her now when she needed them most? A tiny germ of an unpleasant idea crept into Gemma's mind. This was her parents' fault for not being there for her when she most needed them. But she quickly stamped out the idea. It was not their fault. It was the fault of the man who had abducted her. His and no one else's.

Then, it might have been morning, or maybe it was later the same evening, he stood in the doorway again, wearing only his dressing gown. Gemma knew what was coming.

"I'm gong to have a quick shower," he announced in the usual casual and strangely pleasant manner. Gemma caught a glimpse of his smile.

"Okay," she responded with a false calm. In her mind, she talked to her reflection in the mirror in her bedroom, "We can get through this," her own image told her. "Find something to focus on. Give it 100 per cent of our attention."

Gemma's eyes strayed around the room. On a table at the other end of the room was what looked like a plain glass fruit bowl. Gemma found herself suddenly aware of a slight glimmer. She could not quite make it out. Perhaps it was a flaw in the glass; more probably, it was spider's web. Maybe it was a dandelion seed, caught on a spider's web. Why, she asked herself was she thinking about that instead of her dangerous situation. It didn't matter. Now Gemma had something to focus on. She conjured in her mind a meadow with lush green grass and dandelions, lots of yellow dandelions.

Before she knew it the man was back. He slipped off the dressing gown, smiled gently at her and stroked her long hair off her face. Gemma tried not to flinch. She focussed her mind on the dandelion meadow

"I'm so glad you're mine. I love you so much."

He kissed her gently on the face, neck and breasts. She was in that imaginary meadow with the dandelions.

The man slid his body over her, and started kissing her again.

Gemma had an image of herself in that meadow, still naked, but that didn't matter. She was alone. She was free. She knew what she had to do. She started running. There were no sounds except the beating of her heart and the rhythmic pounding of her bare feet on the ground.

> *Pound, pound, pound.*
> She didn't know where she was going....
> *Pound, pound, pound.*
> It didn't matter…
> *Pound, pound, pound.*
> because the meadow was endless.
> *Pound, pound, pound.*
> The sun was warm.
> *Pound, pound, pound.*
> There wasn't the slightest breeze.
> *Pound, pound, pound.*

After just a little while Gemma stopped running for a moment. She was breathing rapidly now. The dandelions had all lost their colour and had turned to seeds. For some reason a gust of wind that Gemma did not feel whipped up the dandelion seeds. Millions of them formed a cloud that swirled around her. As each one touched her skin it tickled gently sending soft tingles of delight through every inch of her skin, every inch of her body. She had never felt so wonderful. She wanted the moment to last forever.

"I knew you would enjoy that."

Gemma's smile vanished instantly. She was back in reality: A strong chain still held her to a bed and her captor had just raped her again. All the pleasure of experiencing her first orgasm was gone in an instant. She hated him. She hated herself.

CHAPTER SEVEN:

ESCAPE

The fresh air of freedom is so sweet.

Sgt Alan Redwood, *Escape from a Stalag*, 1964

After what seemed a long time, he was at the door again, but this time it was to bring her a cup of hot chocolate, again in a paper cup. Gemma found herself thinking, 'It must be night time.' But she could not be sure. 'I have got to keep track of time,' she told herself. But she was not sure how she was going to do that.

"Thanks," she said but the grudge in her voice was obvious, at least it was to Gemma. A little later Gemma was dozing lightly when she heard him come into the room again. She was instantly wide awake and fully alert, but she feigned sleep. The man had not stopped at the door. Gemma sensed him standing over her. Gently, he pulled the blanket up a little to cover Gemma's naked shoulder. He switched off the light and quietly closed the door.

Gemma was dreaming and for some reason she knew it was a dream. She was sitting beside a large old-fashioned trunk and in it she placed a gun, a bottle of poison and a rope noose. 'Silly', she thought to herself, 'Where would I get a gun? How can I use a rope on him? How can I make him drink poison?' She shivered and realised that the room was freezing cold, so cold that large icicles were hanging from the ceiling. Icicles? Good idea. She broke one off and put it in the trunk with the other weapons. Then she locked the trunk and put the key on the chain round her neck, but it was not the light chain that usually held the medallion that Gemma often wore. It was a heavy metal chain, like the one that still held her prisoner. She woke gently but the idea of an icicle weapon was firmly in her mind.

She found it almost impossible to focus her thoughts. She was too terrified to think clearly. She did not quite understand this because she had always been good at focussed thinking. Years of playing games with Catriona and just being with her had helped sharpen her mind to all manner of things around her.

At home Gemma kept a diary. She logged day-to-day events, but she also included her daily thoughts; random thoughts that one day she would go through and sort into some form of order and use for writing stories or some such thing. She wasn't yet sure. She just liked doing it. What, she wondered, would she be keying into her electronic notebook on her computer right now if she had access to it.

She again drifted into sleep, peppered with thoughts, half thoughts, mixed thoughts, allsorts of thoughts. She had an image, a still image, of Christ on the cross. But she was close, too close. This image was framed by part of the crossbar of the cross and part of the vertical beam. A Roman spear had just stabbed Christ and was dripping blood on to the ground. In the background, there was a green hill below a blue sky. Among the dandelions, where Christ's blood dripped on to the grass, there grew a rose bush with blood red flowers. Gemma woke with this powerful image on her mind. Her mum went to church from time to time, but Gemma did not. But if ever there was a time for faith in some all-good powerful being able to help her, it was now (1).

The man came in with some cornflakes, again in a paper plate and some warm coffee in a paper cup. "Morning," he greeted her cheerily. Gemma did not respond. 'Morning,' she thought to herself. 'God, it must be Sunday morning. Mum will be at church praying for me. I hope it works.'

Her ideas drifted back to embryonic plans to escape. It seemed impossible. Nothing worthwhile came to her mind. She thought of her dad again. He was an engineer. He was clever. He would be able to break the chain at the weakest link or fiddle with the lock to open it.

She thought of Catriona. She would know what to do. She would have a plan. Catriona was smart, always much smarter than Gemma. She could always spot a flaw in the plot of a film or a book. She was always good at solving puzzles. Yes, Catriona would have worked out a plan by now. But just what would she do to escape?

Escape. Yes there was great grandfather Alexander Dusek. He escaped from the Nazis. He would have a plan. He would escape.

Gemma knew that escape was essential if she was to stay alive. She knew that she was not going to get out of the chain by her own efforts. She needed something else. Somehow, she had to persuade the monster to unlock the bonds restraining her.

Slowly, ever so slowly, an idea began to grow. It was a potentially dangerous idea, but it was the only plan that Gemma had. Her mind drifted slowly back to mum and dad. She started to lose concentration. Dam. Had the man put something in the coffee to make her drowsy? She desperately wanted to hold on to the thoughts and memories of mum and dad. She desperately tried to pull them back, but her mind drifted on and into the land of dreams where anything impossible becomes easy.

She had been dozing lightly, thinking over her almost impossible idea of escape, but she was jolted awake by the familiar figure in the dressing gown standing, as before, in the doorway.

"I'm going to have a quick shower," he droned.

Gemma decided to take the risk that she had been thinking about.

"Fine then," she snapped at him. "You go for a shower. . . and *then* come back for me. Don't bother about *me*, waiting here for you. You're a boring old fart anyway. It's always the same with you: Quick shower, quick bit of sex and then off to watch your film or whatever. And it's always the same sex." Gemma paused. She could not concentrate on his reaction. Instead, she was almost congratulating herself, wondering just where her little speech had come from. She jolted her mind. Concentrate she ordered herself.

The man was lost for words.

Gemma continued, "Let's do something different this time. Why don't you start by letting me share the shower with you? Maybe I could show you something new." Her voice had moved swiftly from scolding him to tempting him. She had practised it in her mind. She smiled temptingly.

She watched his face for any signs of a response. It looked like he was thinking it over. After a moment that seemed like an eternity the man made a low rhythmic grunting noise that could have been a threat or could equally have been a suppressed laugh. He moved towards the bed. Gemma wasn't sure if he would batter her for being so stupid, or if he would unlock the chain.

He fumbled for something: a key. Click. For the first time in, well, Gemma didn't know how long, she was not chained, not restrained. Her mind raced. She had to play this deception until the next opportunity arose. She had a few ideas but no real plan beyond this stage. It depended on too many unknown factors.

He led her, willingly, into the bathroom. They stepped into the shower cubicle together and as soon as he had put the water on he turned to face her. A foolish grin spread across the man's face.

He held her close to him, too close. Gemma suddenly wanted to vomit. This was the creature who had held her as a prisoner and had repeatedly raped her, but she had to play this properly. At least the fresh water on her face was keeping her awake. She felt more alert than at any other time in this man's house.

"Have you any shampoo?" Her voice was sweet and innocent.

The man's grin faded. "You want to wash your hair?"

Gemma looked straight into his cold steel grey, almost hypnotic eyes and smiled as sweetly as she could in the circumstances. She slid a single finger gently over his shoulder.

She put on the most sultry, sensuous voice she could. "It's not for my hair, you silly boy."

The man made another grunting noise and his silly grin returned. He found the shampoo and handed Gemma the plastic bottle. Even as he let go of the bottle he had the idea that this was an incredibly stupid thing to do, but he pushed that idea out of his mind.

Gemma poured a generous amount of shampoo into one hand. He looked at it. She looked at him, smiling. What happened next took less than a second. The man didn't see it coming; didn't know at first what had happened.

All he felt was searing pain, blinding pain. By the time he realised that the girl had thrown shampoo into his eyes, she had already stepped out of the shower cubicle. She twisted the lid off the shampoo bottle and squirted as much of it as possible on the tiled floor.

The man reached the wash hand basin without stepping on any of the shampoo. He was throwing handfuls of cold water into his stinging eyes.

Gemma had one thought. Get out of that house. She reached the front door in an instant. It was locked, but the key was in the lock. As she turned it, she heard the monster behind her.

"Where are you, bitch. I'm going to fucking kill you. Where are you?"

Gemma had the front door open. The man was fumbling his way along the hall. His head was bleeding and he was limping. Clearly he had fallen on the bathroom floor. The shampoo trap had worked.

He was still blinded by the shampoo in the eyes. Gemma saw an untidy shelf at the front door with boots, and an umbrella with what looked like a heavy handle. An idea flashed into her mind and she grabbed the umbrella.

"Fuck you. Where are you?"

"Right here."

The man stopped and turned. Gemma swung the umbrella and gave the man a hard smack across the face sending out a spray of blood and a part of a tooth. A second knock hit him hard in the groin. He let out a bellow like a wounded animal. As he fell to his knees, his eyes opened and Gemma could see that they were severely bloodshot.

The man wheezed, but did not have time to articulate any words. A third knock landed squarely on the back of the head.

The man was semi-conscious. Gemma now took a moment to step back into the room that had been her prison. She picked up the dressing gown the man had draped across her bed before leading her to the shower. Gemma quickly wrapped it round herself.

She left the room, and in just a couple of strides was past the bleeding grunting man. She was at the front door, one step from freedom. She turned back and looked at the semi-conscious body in front of her. She gave it another hard batter in the genitals with the umbrella handle. The whole body gave an involuntary jerk and folded with another agonised grunt.

Then, free at last, Gemma ran through the front door, unsure of the hour of the day and no longer sure, even, of the day of the week, hoping, just hoping that someone would be there, someone who could call for help.

Gemma had very clear memories of everything that had happened in Stansfield's house, but the hours that followed her escape had become rather fuzzy.

She remembered running out of the house and along the road... a woman giving help; questions; the police; questions; a horrible intimate examination by a sympathetic lady doctor; questions, sympathy, questions and more questions. The same questions, over and over again; then at last, home and family.

She was not sure how long she had been a prisoner for but to Gemma it seemed to have been an eternity.

Gemma's parents, Catriona, someone from the social work department and a couple of police officers produced a strange mix of emotions: relief that Gemma was home; bitter anger at what had been done to her and just about everything in between.

Quite suddenly Gemma did not want to be there. While she had been imprisoned all she wanted was to be safe with her family. Now there were too many people around, all she wanted was solitude. She wanted to have a bath. She slipped quietly out of the room and went upstairs.

Hardly anyone spoke and when they did it was in whispers, as if they were attending a funeral.

Catriona heard one of the police officers asking her mum if she was sure Gemma would be all right on her own.

Catriona was certain that she would be. Gemma was strong enough not to cause herself any harm, but she quickly and quietly slipped out of the room and up the stairs.

Catriona knocked on the bathroom door and without waiting for answer went in.

Gemma was hunched up in the bath but had not filled it with water. The shower was on but Gemma was in the lee of the spray and was hardly wet. Her knees were pulled tightly to her and her arms were wrapped round them. She had been sobbing again, but now she had no tears left.

She looked at Catriona with reddened eyes and gave a tiny nod of the head which Catriona took to mean, 'Thanks for coming in.'

"Are you all right?" Catriona asked with a shaking voice. As soon as she said it, she wished she had not asked. It was a stupid question. Of course Gemma was not all right. Not now; maybe at some time far in the future, but not right now.

"Sorry", she added softly. Gemma did not answer.

"Gem, he's going to jail. They'll lock him up for years and years."

Slowly Gemma turned to Catriona and gave a weak smile. Catriona picked up a large bath towel and wrapped it around Gemma as she stood up.

Ten minutes later they joined the family downstairs, Gemma, looking a little bit more like herself.

The man who had abducted and raped Gemma was Richard Graham Mackenzie Stansfield. He was arrested immediately, packed off to the accident and emergency unit at Knadger House Hospital and kept under observation by both medical staff and the police.

Stansfield was jailed for ten years. After his release he found it too difficult to cope with his guilt. Eventually his mental sickness got the better of him and he ended up in the mental health unit at Craigmark Hospital.

Maria felt angry and betrayed by Stansfield. She told the girls, that like The Rev Lucas, she had thought that Stansfield was a simple and gentle soul. There had been nothing in Stansfield's files about any of this; nothing about him having been in prison.

Gemma asked Maria about the one thing that had been seriously worrying her, but she cautiously edged around it.

"You said that you thought he was married. You mentioned that he kept a diary."

Gemma and Catriona knew it was odd, because they both knew that Stansfield was barely able to write anything. Catriona deliberately used the word 'diary' instead of notebook. She felt that by wrongly describing it, they would be disguising their very keen interest in it and in what Stansfield might have written.

Maria looked at them a little vaguely. "Oh that. No. I checked that out I don't think he was ever married and his notebook is just some incoherent rambling. You know, stuff like, 'Someone stole my house.' I think the police were right, there's nothing important in his notebook. Stansfield lived in a past of his own making."

After their meeting with Maria, Gemma raised the issue of the notebook again with her sister. "I wonder what Maria has done with the notebook. It could still cause us problems."

Catriona was more positive, "I doubt it. We don't know what's in it, but no one is taking it seriously - *Someone stole my house*," She repeated in a rather silly voice. "Would you take it seriously?"

Gemma and Catriona laughed together. Gemma added, "It's a bit odd though. If Stansfield had not written it and if Maria had not mentioned it to me, we would never have told her any of that."

CHAPTER EIGHT

THE LONG AND WINDING ROAD

The body will always heal swifter than the mind.

The Rev Colin Lyndhurst,
Heart and Soul, 1922.

Having told Maria as much of the events as they dared, Gemma and Catriona thought that that would be the end of it all, but wasn't.

Mandy Stafford had the link, that very early link between Richard Graham Mackenzie Stansfield and Gemma Dusk. In her hand she again held that scribbled note from her file. The information on it had never been made public. It would have been illegal to make it public at the time. On a sheet torn from her notebook and now languishing in her Stansfield file, Mandy had written: *Rape victim, Gemma Dusk, 15.* She could no longer remember, but it must have come from a police or court contact. She had not sourced the information at the time. It was not important then. It was probably not important now.

Now that Stansfield was dead, there was no point in bringing it all up again. In any case, there was something else to consider about Gemma Dusk. That leaflet promoting her exhibition had Gemma's painting of Glenbank Cottage on it. That was a loose end and Mandy Stafford hated loose ends.

Glenbank, Glenbank, Mandy kept turning it over in her head. Something lurking deep in the back of her mind told her that at one time she had either written about Glenbank or had at least taken notes on the cottage. Perhaps it was some notes that had never quite materialised into a story, and yet she had found nothing filed under Glenbank in either the cuttings file in the office or in her own notes file. What was it? She let her mind drift, which was always a useful technique to help clear it of the clutter of the day. She could not be sure of the details, but she became certain that it had something to do with an impossible event. Mandy thought of checking her file on mysteries, always a good place for wacky things.

She pulled out her notes on mysteries and the first one she found was about her cousin, Sandi Forde, now an archaeologist. Mandy smiled. She and Sandi had the same flaming red hair. A long time ago, Sandi had told her a strange tale. She had been in Masterman's Collectables shop when she picked up a medal and had a sudden flash, or vision, of it being presented to a boy in a swimming costume. Sandi dropped it immediately saying there was something wrong with it, but another customer had picked it up and had shown no reaction at all. Very strange, but not at all helpful.

Mandy checked other files but found nothing. Then just as she was about to close the filing cabinet drawer she spotted it... a file marked Bank Glen. With eager hands she searched it and found what she had been looking for. It was just a couple of pages of notes from a police contact and it concerned a rather confused and frightened young man who had come into the police office and claimed that his car and his house had been stolen. Her notes confirmed that the man was Richard Graham Mackenzie Stansfield and Mandy immediately realised, the house was not Bank Glen as logged in her notebook of the time, but Glenbank.

That was curious. Mandy made some checks and the case became even more curious. The painting of Glenbank in the exhibition leaflet was dated March, 2007 but that date meant that the painting was dated between Stansfield's release from Bowhouse Prison and his admission to Craigamark Hospital. It was a time when Stansfield had been living at Glenbank Cottage, and Gemma Dusk must have known that when she made the painting. The isolated link had been strengthened. At last Mandy had the hint of a story. She did not know yet what the story was, but she was sure there was something there.

She planned to speak to Gemma as soon as possible, but before she did so, she wanted to prepare the ground. The best questions a reporter can ask, she always felt, are the ones that they already have answers to. Reactions to questions speak louder than the answers. Mandy once again sifted through her files on both Stansfield and Gemma Dusk, this time making notes.

When Mandy phoned Gemma she had enough common sense not to mention the rape and abduction but she did say that she found it rather odd that Gemma had painted Glenbank Cottage at a time when Richard Graham Mackenzie Stansfield was living there. Gemma was taken by surprise, but she had enough presence of mind to say that it was not a good time to talk and could they meet face-to-face. Gemma claimed that she would be visiting her parents in Dunmerick in a couple of days. Mandy fixed a time and place. After this call, Gemma phoned her parents and invited herself to the family home. Then she called Catriona.

The three of them, Mandy, Gemma and Catriona met in Drouthy Tam's in Castle Road. It was a modern superpub, part of a large national pub chain and almost midway between the commercial centre of Dunmerrick and the old castle around which the original town had started to grow. It was a popular place, but one that Gemma said had factory art on the walls and factory food on the plates. Mandy agreed with Gemma about food and the art, but this pub had booths where they could talk more or less privately and it had a good selection of real ales.

On the wall of the booth there was a poster advertising a forthcoming event with cLIVE MUSIC, from Clive Crockett.

"I used to date him," Mandy told the girls in an attempt to break the ice, and she added that Clive occasionally returned to perform in Dunmerrick.

Getting no response from the sisters, she added. "Nice chap, but it didn't work out between us."

There was an awkward silence. And Mandy started talking about the purpose of the meeting, raising the point about the painting of the cottage at a time Stansfield was living there and its subsequent demolition which seemed to have been one of the factors that finally unhinged Stansfield.

Gemma and Catriona had already agreed that they were going to tell Mandy what they had told Maria, but they knew that Mandy would be more thorough and more inquisitive than Maria and they knew that they might have to tell her a lot more.

They were right. In what felt like a recurring nightmare, they told Mandy the same as they had told Maria. But when Mandy started questioning them again about the cottage, they told her the rest of the story.

The version of the bathroom conversation that Gemma and Catriona had given to Maria O'Connell had not quite been the whole truth.

As soon as possible after getting home from her ordeal, all Gemma wanted to do was take a bath.

Catriona came into the bathroom. Gemma was hunched up in the bath, knees pulled tightly to her and her arms wrapped round them.

"Are you all right?" Catriona asked with a shaking voice and she quickly added, "Sorry", in a more loving voice.

It took Gemma what seemed to be an age to respond. At last she told Catriona what she had not told her parents; not the doctor and definitely not the police.

Gemma spoke slowly with some long pauses. She chose her words carefully. She did not look at her sister while she was speaking and her eyes were strangely unfocussed. Catriona had the love and the patience not to interrupt, not even with a gasp and not to push for more information. She listened intently.

"I wanted to kill him….. I tried to kill him… but I couldn't do it. Oh, I gave him a battering. He was nearly unconscious. I took the chord from his dressing gown. It… It should have been easy. I wrapped it round his neck and I pulled it tight.

"I remember saying, 'Die, you sick bastard, die.' But I just didn't have the strength to kill him."

And after another long silent pause Gemma added, "I still want to kill him. I've even thought out how to do it."

"Gem, he's going to jail. They'll lock him up for years."

"I'll make a spike out of ice... I'll follow him and I'll stick it in the back of his filthy head."

"Gemma, they'll send him to jail for years and years."

"That's not enough. By the time they find his body the ice will have melted. They'll never find the weapon."

"Gem, listen to me. They would find you. They would send *you* to jail."

"I don't care."

"*I* care Catriona snapped. But her anger was fake. The shout had been a calculated attempt to get Gemma's train of thought back to some form of reality.

"Dam it, Gem, you need a better plan than that... something so good that they will never be able trace it back to us. Anyway, death's too good for him."

"And what about your plan to become a lawyer? If we get caught...

"Fuck that. You're more important," Catriona shouted in anger, but it was again a carefully controlled mock anger.

Gemma had never heard her sister swear like this before, but the phrase that had caught her attention was, 'they will never trace it back to us.'

'*To us*,' seemed to echo in Gemma's mind. Gemma turned to look at her sister and asked in a flat voice: "You got a better plan?"

"Not yet, Gem. But I promise I will. We'll get him together."

And for the first time since they were re-united, Gemma gave a smile, a weak smile, but one that Catriona accepted as meaning OK.

Slowly Gemma held out her right hand with her little finger extended. Catriona took it in her little finger and they shook to agree the deal.

Catriona picked up a large bath towel and wrapped it around Gemma as she stood up.

Ten minutes later they joined the family downstairs. Gemma was looking a little bit more like herself. She put on a forced smile, almost a grimace and started to mingle with the house full of people. She had already met Sgt Mathieson, who while retaining her complete professionalism as a police officer, was also sympathetic and supportive.

Gemma was introduced to Barry Wainwright from the social work department. He had been allocated to her case and would help her on the long road to recovery.

Gemma felt weary. Now all she wanted to do was go to her own bed and have a long deep sleep without the fear.

Gemma's road to recovery was not a smooth one. It was her Long and Winding Road, as she called it, after a song by the Beatles.

A few days after she came home from her ordeal Gemma was sitting at her bedroom table staring silently at her reflection. The radio was playing some music, but Gemma wasn't listening to it. She was thinking of what had happened in Hudson Park that afternoon when she had been out with Catriona.

They had been sitting at the Freedom Monument. This tall stone pillar, also known as the Slavery Monument, is set in a small square with benches around it. The platform on the top of the pillar has no figure on it, for all men and women are equal in the eyes of God. The monument's central position of the park and it being a focal point made it a natural and popular meeting place.

The girls were looking at the four inscriptions on the sides of the square base. One reads *'All men are created equal'* and the next has a quote from Robert Burns, *A man's a man for a' that*. There is another quote from Robert Burns on a third panel, *Man's inhumanity to man makes countless thousands mourn.*

The main panel has an explanation of the monument. 'This monument is dedicated to the memory of American Abolitionist Frederick Douglass who visited this town in April, 1846, and to all those he inspired to work for the freedom of all people. April,1898' (1).

Gemma and Catriona were considering the monument and the right thinking people of late 19th century Dunmerrick when a group of boys passed. The boys turned to look at them. Gemma was suddenly terrified and she instinctively grasped Catriona's sleeve.

Thinking about it even moments later, Gemma realised that her action had been silly. The boys had not threatened them in any way. They had just turned to look at two pretty girls. That was all.

Gemma looked at her reflection. She knew she was beautiful. Had several of her male friends not told her she was beautiful. Had the rapist not said, 'You have lovely hair.'

Gemma did not know how long she sat staring at her own (beautiful) reflection, looking into her own dark brown eyes, but the longer she did the more she also reflected on the events that had traumatised her and the more she thought of that, the more she knew that she did want to be so beautiful any more.

She glanced at the scissors on the table. 'Yes', she thought, 'It was my fault. I'm too pretty. No, no. Not my fault.' And she pushed that terrible thought away to somewhere in her mind that it could be locked away forever.

She looked at the scissors again. She did not want boys chasing after her. Not now. Not ever. She looked at the scissors and let her eyes slide along their shining blades.

Slowly, cautiously, Gemma reached out. Her hand hovered over the scissors for a moment. She picked them up with a slightly trembling hand. After a moment of self-doubt, she began cutting her beautiful hair to be short, boyish.

Those first few cuts were made with care, but with tears starting to well in her eyes and with an almost steely determination the cutting became less focussed.

Beautiful long strands fell carelessly to the floor and in some places, the short hair that was left, stuck out at odd angles.

Gemma put down the scissors and for a while stared unseeing, at her own reflection.

It was just a little later that Catriona came into Gemma's room. She was shocked. She had always loved the natural beauty of Gemma's long black curly hair and the way it could shimmer in the light. Even when they where younger, Catriona had sat brushing Gemma's hair, saying how beautiful it was. But Catriona had enough sense and enough love for her sister not to make an issue of this. She refrained from scolding Gemma too much. Her look said it all and Gemma knew what her sister was thinking.

"I'm not very good at recovery," Gemma said softly, with the start of tears still in her eyes.

The voice on the radio was between songs. "This one is for Rosie Beattie. The message is from your dad. He says… 'I know you have had some tough times recently, but just remember, I will always be here for you. You'll never be alone.'

"Isn't that sweet. Well, good luck, Rosie, whatever your troubles are and what else could we play for you but this classic from Gerry and the Pacemakers."

The girls had not really been listening, but they immediately warmed to the lyrics. The song seemed to speak to them, and them alone.

When you walk through a storm,
Hold your head up high,
And don't be afraid of the dark.

The girls exchanged glances. They were thinking the same thing. Gemma had certainly been through a storm. She was still in the dark. As the song progressed the girls paid more attention to the words. Four eyes in that room were now sparkling with tears. As the song reached its crescendo both girls had tears streaming down their faces.

Walk On! With hope in your heart,
And you'll never walk alone....

Gemma and Catriona both had smiles on their tear-stained faces as they hugged and in doing so they silently sealed the tentative deal they had made a few days before.

"Gemma," Catriona whispered softly, "Your hair doesn't matter. You are still beautiful. You hold your head up high and I will always... always, be here for you."

With some gentle persuasion Catriona persuaded Gemma to make an appointment with Michael at Hizz and Hairs in Portland Drive.

Michael was distressed to see what Gemma had done to her (beautiful) hair and he told her so, but he was professional enough and careful enough not to criticise her and not to ask about the reasons she had done it. Instead while he worked at repairing as much of the damage as he could, he assured Gemma that given some time her hair would grow back and be as good as ever. That, in his opinion, is what she should do... let it grow long again.

Gemma left Hizz and Hairs feeling just a little better about herself but determined to keep her hair short. She did not want boys attracted by her beautiful hair.

Gemma's mum, Samantha, was a shift supervisor at a large supermarket and was used to being in charge of people, but ever since Gemma got home, she had been making a bit too much of a fuss over Gemma, wanting to make her cups of tea or coffee, telling her to relax, offering to do her washing, offering cups of tea, coffee, tea and more tea, not to mention the biscuits and cakes.

Eventually Gemma snapped at her mum, yelling at her she was fine, which, of course, she wasn't, and telling her to leave her alone. She regretted it at once. She had never argued with her mum before, never snapped at her before and seeing the shocked look on her mum's face she apologised immediately, and got up and hugged her. Both women had tears in their eyes. There were a lot of tears in the Dusk family home in the weeks after Gemma returned.

Gemma's dad, Alexander, was an engineer and a very practical man. He was always easy-going, but Gemma's experience had left him feeling bitter and angry. A couple of days after she got home when the household had started to return to what seemed to be a normal routine, he quietly pulled Gemma aside.

"I want to get him," he told her. "I have a plan. We grab him like he grabbed you; chain him to a chair facing into a corner in a basement room. Keep the lights on all the time. Feed him at odd times, so he doesn't know if it's night or day. We go into the room and stand behind him… talk about how to dispose of him. It'll drive him nuts."

Gemma was smart enough to dismiss the idea at once and she repeated to her dad what Catriona had told her, "Dad, he's going to jail. They'll lock him up for years and years."

Gemma sounded convincing but she did not really mean it. She was certainly not going to let the matter rest with a simple jail sentence that would almost certainly be too short. She and Catriona had already started talking about 'a better plan.' They still did not know exactly what that plan would be but they did not want their dad mixed up in anything illegal. Even so, the suggestion from their dad that they could drive Stansfield nuts had a certain appeal and an idea began to grow.

A few days after the incident at the Freedom Monument, Catriona had, with some difficulty, persuaded Gemma to take a trip into town, 'Just for a coffee or an ice cream,' she had said, though she didn't really mean it. She was keen to get Gemma out of the house where, in Catriona's view, she was spending too much time moping about.

Gemma had agreed. They went into town and had just emerged from Mastermans having bought nothing, when Gemma noticed something in the window. Her face unexpectedly broke into a smile. Catriona asked why, but her question went unanswered and Gemma simply said she would only be a minute. She went into the shop again and came out a few minutes later, having bought a dartboard.

"I'm going to get a picture of Stansfield and throw darts at his horrible face. Do you think I could learn voodoo?"

Catriona was not quite sure how to take this suggestion, but as things turned out, Gemma never did attach a picture of Stansfield's face to her dartboard and she never did take the suggestion of learning voodoo any further.

More than anything else, Gemma was dreading going back to Dunmerrick Academy. Her biggest fear was that everyone would know what had happened to her and they would all want to talk to her about it and ask her so many questions. It would be the same questions, over and over again.

To help Gemma recover, it was decided to keep her off school for at least a week. Mum and dad decided to put it about that Gemma had a bout of flu. Catriona objected, saying that the deception was weak. There was no flu around, but her objection was overruled.

Mum, dad and Catriona all tried hard to distract Gemma from her trauma and on the Saturday before she had to return to school, the family took Gemma to Glasgow.

They happened to visit the Gallery of Modern Art. Gemma had a casual interest in art at this time. The visit laid a seed in Gemma's mind, one that would change her whole life, two seeds really. It made her think for the first time that she might be able to take art as a certificate subject at school. It would be better to work alone instead of being part of a team.

One of her first pieces of art, though she didn't think of it that way at the time, was also inspired by the visit to the Gallery of Modern Art.

In a display case there was an umbrella, and instead of rain falling on to it, there were words landing on it. The umbrella, instead of acting as a shield was acting more like a word processor, for coming out from beneath its cover, there were sentences.

Gemma was fascinated by this piece of modern art and it inspired her to do something unusual with her new dartboard. She stripped off the metal wire numbers and dividers and she asked her engineer dad to rig up a system that would allow her to turn the dartboard one number segment at a time. Dad was happy to help.

With the rotating dartboard in place on the wall of her bedroom, Gemma went through some newspapers and magazines looking for a selection of words, but each one had to be just the right word. She cut out 'hope' and pasted it on to the first of the segments of the dartboard. It would not be the last word that she pasted on to what she soon came to call her Mood Wheel.

Gemma stood outside the school building, holding back as the rush of other students went inside when the bell rang, but she could not wait too long.

Gemma's fears about being the centre of attention turned out to be unfounded. Quite a few of her classmates commented on her hair, but that was all. After registration she had a meeting with the head teacher, Mr Fergus McLean, who had been in teaching for several decades and was now coasting towards retirement. She was told that only a few selected senior members of staff knew that she had been the victim of such a horrible crime. She was assured that every effort would be made to protect her privacy, every support would be given to her and she was further assured that if there was anything the school could do to help her, it would be done.

Two days later, having given a lot of thought to this proposal, Gemma was back in Mr McLean's office. She explained that she no longer wanted to be part of the athletics team or the swimming team.

Gemma craved the idea of something that she could do on her own. She had always been good at art and asked if she could change to art as a certificate subject in place of PT. Her request was quickly approved, perhaps out of sympathy, or perhaps because it was felt that this would help her recovery. Gemma's new art teacher was Frank Hastings. He did not know the reasons for Gemma's sudden interest in taking art as a certificate subject. He did not need to know. He respected every individual student and he tried hard to encourage the wide variety of talents his students had.

Mr Hastings was tall and slim. He had long untidy grey hair… silver, he called it. He was usually dressed in old clothes, though this was just for art classes. When required, he could dress smartly.

'Be yourself.' He would tell them. 'Look at the way the art establishment treated Jack Vettriano.'

Mr Hastings had no great respect for the exam system. Gemma remembered him saying something like, 'these bloody exams just want to mould you into the system. Buck the system.' That's how Gemma chose to remember it, but he might have said something else. He was the only teacher Gemma ever heard using swear words in front of the class. All the students loved him.

Having secured a place in the art class, Gemma looked out her Mood Wheel and added 'Happy'.

Frank Hastings was one of the most patient teachers Gemma had ever met. He immediately recognised that Gemma had an exceptional talent. In discussions before putting any paint on canvas, Gemma would float ideas of images, symbolism and visual puns. On one occasion she told him, "I would like to paint something about temptations."

"Ah, chocolate," Mr Hastings responded with a wry smile.

"No, no. Darker temptations."

"You mean dark chocolate," he responded with a sarcastic smile.

They laughed at this. They each knew exactly what the other meant. Artistically they were on the same wavelength.

Under his guidance, Gemma produced her first canvas. He had been telling Gemma, as the new student in the certificate grade class, that the world was a wonderful carousel of colour. But it so happened that there had been a fog the previous night and Gemma said she wanted to paint that.

This, her first full painting in that class, was called Fogbound. The painting went on to win a lot of praise and a national prize. In response, Gemma stuck the word 'excellence' on her Mood Wheel in what she called a triple word score.

In an interview years later, when Gemma had become a renowned painter, Mr Hastings said that his favourite piece of work from Gemma was one which featured paratroopers emerging from an aircraft. On their descent they turned into dandelion seeds, but as each one approached the ground it turned into a snowflake… *a moment white, then melts forever* (2).

Gemma met up with Barry Wainwright from the social work department on several occasions, but she found him unhelpful. He constantly told her that the past can't be undone.

"Think of it like a bereavement," he would say. "It's something you have gone through, and now you have to get over it."

Just get over it! That's easy to say, Gemma thought, but how do you get over something that has traumatised you? Barry Wainwright never come across as a friend. He gave the impression of someone who was working a case in accordance to a pre-planned script. He did not discuss matters outside his own work zone. They talked about Gemma's recovery and that was all. No chit chat, no informal references to the weather or anything else for that matter. As far as Gemma could see, there was not even any real sympathy there. During her meetings with him, Gemma came across as rather sullen… and Barry Wainwright put this down to the impact that the abduction and rape had had on her. It was something Gemma just had to work hard at to get over. Just get over it!

Thinking about him, Gemma added 'loser' to her Mood Wheel, this time giving it a double word score.

In Catriona's company, Gemma would light up, like her old self and if talking to Catriona about Barry Wainwright, Gemma took to calling him Weary Brain Right. After one particularly irksome session with him, Gemma thought about her Mood Wheel and moaned, "He's a loser. He's a loser with a capital L. If had had come from Wales he would have had two capital Ls." Catriona smiled then laughed. Gemma found that her anger quickly dissolved and she was laughing too.

She and Catriona talked about anything, everything. If they did drift back to the subject of Stansfield, they took delight in devising new methods of getting revenge when he came out of Bowhouse Prison. Most of the revenge ideas were pure fantasy. Most, but not all.

CHAPTER NINE

TO RECOVERY

Everybody needs something to hope for.

- Maitland Reeves, *From Darkness Into Light*, 1970.

Gemma went along to a meeting of the local Rape Crisis group. She was reluctant, but she had been pressured into going by Barry, her mum, dad and in more subtle ways, Catriona.

Catriona went with her to that first meeting. When they arrived, Gemma was apprehensive, scared even. She did not want to have to go over all those events yet again.

But after she arrived and held out a metaphorical hand, she found it taken gently. She was embraced by a group of women who did not want to pry, but just wanted to give her whatever support they could. They embraced her as a friend. And Gemma found that she could, after all, talk to the women in this group, despite the fact that they were strangers, about what had happened to her in ways that she could never have talked, Barry. Of course, they were women who understood. Barry Wainwright was just another man.

Home again and Gemma added the word 'positive' to her Mood Wheel.

The day after that first meeting of the Rape Crisis group, Catriona took Gemma to the Drunken Sailor for lunch and for the first time they started making more serious and more practical plans for getting revenge on Stansfield. They decided that there was little that they could do without knowing a lot more about him. They needed to find out everything they could. They had to know his strong points and his weak points. They could not plan anything without proper information about the enemy.

The police kept in touch with Gemma, early on, almost on a daily basis, occasionally asking for clarification on some part of her statement. These talks were held at Gemma's home and were always informal.

But one day one of the officers who had come to speak to her said something which caused her some anguish.

"You do realise that we can't take sides. That in effect it is your word against his." Gemma had not even thought that her word would be seriously questioned. She had been abducted and raped.

"Mr Stansfield is still in hospital recovering from various injuries. He says that you attacked him that you nearly blinded him."

Gemma tried desperately to put all this into perspective. "He had me locked up. You must have found the chains."

"He says that that was your idea, your idea of fun."

"I'm only fifteen".

"What about the severe injuries he has? What happened there?"

Gemma thought desperately. She told the police officer that after being chained up she persuaded Stansfield to unlock the chain. He led her to the shower. She remembered holding a shampoo bottle. There was a struggle. Some of the shampoo might have spilled on the floor. Some of it might have splashed in his eyes. Gemma said that all she wanted to do was get out of the house.

The officers left, but Gemma was sure that their investigation was now going in a direction that might put her in serious trouble.

Gemma was in court for Stansfield's trial and she had taken the stand. She was being cross-examined.

"You teased him. Didn't you?"

"No."

"You led him on."

"No."

"You wanted him to have sex with you."

"NO."

"You encouraged him."

"NO I DID NOT."

Stansfield sat in the dock with that silly grin on his face. The same one that he had had just before Gemma had thrown shampoo into his eyes. Gemma saw now that Stansfield's head was bandaged and one and of his eyes was covered with a patch.

"And when you got fed up with him, you attacked him."

"No."

"You nearly blinded him."

"No." Gemma was close to sobbing.

"You attacked him... brutally."

Stansfield sat in front of the dock in his wheelchair, looking quite weak and pathetic.

"And after battering him unconscious, you tried to kill him."

"No," Gemma whispered hoarsely. She was just about defeated. She had no strength left to fight her case.

"You tried to murder him, when all he wanted was a little tender love."

That revived Gemma a little. "NO. HE RAPED ME," Gemma shouted, pointing at the accused.

"Be quiet. Just answer the questions."

"The truth is that you are a thoroughly bad person. It's you who should be going to jail."

"I agree," proclaimed the sheriff. He battered the bench with his little gavel and proclaimed. "I am going to send you to prison."

"Go to jail.

"Go directly to jail.

"Do not pass Go.

"Do not collect £200."

Gemma woke with a start. The dream had unsettled her. For a short while after she had woken up she was more than unsettled. She was terrified, but she hid it well and after she had showered and had breakfast the fear had abated. However, the prospect of a trial did worry Gemma. She would have to come face to face with him again and she would have to relive the nightmare that he had put her through. Later that day she added the word 'Scared' to her Mood Wheel on a double score panel.

The police continued to talk to Gemma, but soon they let her know that they were satisfied with her story. They had enough evidence against Stansfield and would soon go to the Procurator Fiscal, who would take the prosecution case to court.

In time, however, it was reported in the *Dunmerrick Herald* that Stansfield had, through a lawyer, pled guilty to the charges of abduction and rape of an unnamed victim. There would be no trial and there would be no waiting, no reliving the dreadful trauma.

At the High Court, almost six months after the events, Richard Graham Mackenzie Stansfield was packed off to jail for ten years.

When Gemma heard this news, she added 'relief' to the Mood Wheel, on a triple score space.

Rape beast caged said the heading on the story in the *Dunmerrick Herald* and Gemma cut the item from the newspaper.

As there would be no trial, Gemma's belongings were returned to her; her clothes and her handbag containing some loose change, a purse with some banknotes, some cosmetics, pen, pocket diary, some mints, chewing gum and a pair of earrings Gemma had bought shortly before she had been abducted. Curiously, that was the one item she had forgotten about. Gemma checked the contents and confirmed to police everything was in order.

Gemma's latent artistic talents quickly flourished. She threw herself completely into her artwork at school and at home. Her dad cleared out the garden shed, ran an electric cable to it and converted it into a studio. It was far from ideal. At times it was cold and damp and there were spiders, lots of spiders. But it was Gemma's first studio and she loved it. She called it her Art Shed. The word 'haven' was cut from a magazine and added to the Mood Wheel, which was relocated from her bedroom to the Art Shed.

While Gemma painted or while she was looking for inspiration, she played music and she had found that her dad's taste for 1960s music was far more inspiring than music from any other era. The Art Shed often resounded to the sounds of Elvis, The Beatles, The Rolling Stones, Louis Armstrong and many others. Gemma was happy in her Art Shed.

She found inspiration in the most mundane things. Sometimes it was just a word that gave her ideas, or a memory would come up to the surface leaving Gemma bubbling with ideas. Sometimes it was a smell or some object that she had seen. Many of her paintings now represented a bright and positive mood, blue skies, white clouds, green trees and red roses too.

But Gemma had not forgotten the plans that she and Catriona had been discussing and she obtained a steel filing cabinet. This was stored in her studio and it was kept locked at all times. There were only two keys and everyone knew that the contents of the cabinet marked Sister Stuff was out of bounds to all but Gemma and Catriona. Her parents did not know and did not even suspect what was really in the cabinet. They put its existence down to the fact that the girls had always been close, not just sisters, but best friends as well, and they gladly tolerated the distraction of this sibling secrecy.

Gemma started placing anything at all she could find that might be useful in the cabinet, starting with copies of newspaper cuttings about the case and about the road crash that had killed Stansfield's parents. She managed to obtain a copy of Stansfield's school record... it didn't help much, but it was just a little bit extra information that might, or might not prove useful.

Through her studies to become a lawyer, Catriona had built up a group of contacts and friends in legal and police circles. From one of them, she managed to wheedle copies of some police reports, 'just for study', of course. The girls needed to know everything for only then would they know how to slay the dragon.

Over several months, Gemma and Catriona discussed the possibility that the new occupant of Stansfield's home at No 24 Riverside Terrace might know something about him. They did not know if the house had been owned by Stansfield's family or was still a council property.

Gemma did not want to go anywhere near either the building or the street, so Catriona visited the place on her own. The garden outside No 24 was neatly kept. Below the front room window there was bench on which was seated two life-sized knitted figures of young lovers. The boy was presenting the girl with a bunch of real flowers. 'Very artistic' Catriona thought to herself. 'Must tell Gem about that.' (1)

The houses at Riverside Terrace were of two stories and constructed with harled stone. They had been built as council homes in the early 1930s. Some appeared to have changed little since then, but others had been given a make-over, and most of them had satellite dishes. The house at No 24 was an end terrace building, but it was not a full road that separated No 24 from No 26. It was a narrow lane provided for access to the rear of the properties.

Catriona hesitated before ringing the doorbell. She wondered, 'what if the house is now occupied by a long lost relative or maybe a close friend that she and Gemma had failed to find?'

Below the doorbell there was a small tag with Jonathan and Molly McVie printed on it. Catriona stabbed cautiously at the bell button with a slightly trembling finger.

The door was opened almost at once by a woman with a huge smile of impossibly white teeth set against her dark brown skin.

Catriona did not have time to introduce herself before the woman spoke.

"Come in," she invited in a friendly frenzy. "In there," she pointed to a room just off the hallway and hurried on. "I'll be with you in a jiffy."

Her look may have been Jamaican but her accent was pure west of Scotland. Catriona smiled, then silently scolded herself. This might have been the very room in which her sister had been held prisoner and raped.

The host was back in a moment with a tray of pizza slices. Clearly she was expecting someone else.

Catriona stuttered the start of an introduction. "I'm eh...."

"Mandy. From the Herald?"

"No. I'm Catriona."

"Oh. Mandy couldn't manage. Never mind. Eat up."

"No. I'm not from the Herald," Catriona managed to explain at last.

Her host smiled, then laughed. "Help yourself to pizza, anyway. There's plenty more. I was expecting someone from the Herald. They want to do a feature about my people."

Catriona noticed that there were several life-sized knitted people in the room and some appeared to be of well known local people.

"I knit people... well it's a hobby. My real job is at Drouthy Tam's. Do you know it?"

"Yes, out at Castle Road. Look, I've nothing to do with the Herald. I wondered if you knew anything about the man who, lived here before you."

"No. Nothing at all. You should speak to Mr Carter next door. I mean, he's been here forever. And he knows everyone."

The doorbell rang. "Oh. That'll be Mandy from the Herald."

And as Catriona left she thanked Mrs McVie for the pizza and promised she would visit Mr Carter.

Neither Gemma nor Catriona had thought of canvassing the neighbours, but Mr Carter did seem to be the type of person who might know something about Stansfield. *"He's been here forever. And he knows everyone."*

Catriona knocked at the door and waited with mounting apprehension. It was soon opened by a familiar figure… the school janitor. He was just a little bit overweight and had a rather puffy face. He was almost, but not quite bald. It looked as if he hadn't shaved for a day or two.

"Mr Carter?" Catriona asked in surprise. Charles Carter was a popular figure around Dunmerrick Academy where he was head of the janitorial team. He eyed Catriona clearly thinking.

"You're one of the Dusk girls." It was half question, half statement, the type that the mouth speaks while the mind is working hard. "The clever one. Dux medal last year." His tone was pleasant, but it suddenly became severe.

"How is your sister? Terrible business. Shocking."

Clearly Mr Carter was one of the few people who knew the details. Catriona's mind was racing. Of course, as a neighbour he would know more than most.

She gave a rather non-committal response. "She's getting on. I wonder if you could tell me anything about the man from next door."

Mr Carter became rather hesitant. "Well, yes I expect I could. Come in."

He offered Catriona coffee, but he was clearly ill at ease. Had Catriona still been at school, he would never have invited her in, not, on her own anyway.

"That chap was never quite right - a bit simple but not enough to be in care. I think he really lost it when his parents died in a car crash – no excuse for what he did, of course – none. That was horrible."

He was getting into his stride now and Catriona sipped at her coffee listening intently.

"There is something that isn't well known. We, that is, the technical assistants, cover for each other when we have to. Well, last summer just after, you know, well, I was called to the Funmerrick Centre. Stupid name that. I always hated it. You see the parks department have some space inside the building for equipment, grass cutting machines and the like. Well I was called in to plug a hole that had been drilled in the wall there. Now you'll probably already know that Stansfield was working for the parks department. Well whoever drilled the hole had put it at the very place where someone could hide and watch the girls in the changing rooms for the swimming pool."

"Stansfield?"

"I can't prove it, but he had access to that area of the building and it was at that time. It seems to fit what he was like. It was all kept very quiet, of course. Didn't want a lot of parents getting upset, not to mention the girls. Anyway, it doesn't matter now. He's admitted doing what he did to your sister. No need for a trial and he's locked up for a long time."

"Not long enough", muttered Catriona.

Not long after Catriona's visit to Number 24, Gemma and Catriona were in town shopping. They had drifted in to Welbeck Street from Market Square. There was a boutique there that they both liked called Apple Blossom. They had always liked the nice clothes in there. Catriona picked out a T-shirt and held it up for Gemma to see. The slogan on it was 'Drop Dead Gorgeous.'

"This would suit you," Catriona called, across the room. Well, Gemma really was drop dead gorgeous.

She looked at the T-shirt and commented bitterly, "Pity it doesn't say 'Drop dead, Stansfield.'"

Catriona knew she still had a long road ahead to help Gemma on the way to recovery. They went for coffee and Catriona tried distracting Gemma's mind by first talking about art, then making some fantastic, impossible plan to get revenge. They laughed about and it and to Catriona, Gemma's comment seemed to have been an isolated one.

But it was still on Gemma's mind back home the word 'bitter' was added to the Mood Wheel.

Before Gemma left school, her art was good, very good. She had won a national prize and had attracted quite a lot of praise. She knew it was good, but was it good enough for a career?

Gemma still lacked confidence in herself. She was toying with the idea that she could take a course at the Glasgow School of Art, but she was sure that she wasn't good enough.

Dunmerrick Parish Church was planning a spring fayre and through various connections Gemma was asked to put some of her artwork on display. Gemma arrived an hour before the fayre was to be opened. Various tents and stalls were being set up outside the building. Gemma had been given space inside.

The hall was not particularly welcoming. The floor was of plain, unpolished boards. Up to shoulder height, the walls were of the same type of wooden boards, but they had been stained a dark brown colour and were highly polished.

The walls were adorned with the paintings produced by the pre-school children who used the hall most weekday mornings and there was a large notice board, crowded with all sizes of overlapping notices. Quite a few of them announced forthcoming events that had already happened.

Pushed into one corner was a piano and dozens of uncomfortable-looking chairs were stacked along the walls, in piles of five, six and seven chairs.

Gemma was given some free-standing boards on which she could display her paintings. Everyone in the family and at school said her work was excellent, but they would do wouldn't they? Gemma was still highly self-critical.

Gemma had been in the hall for a couple of hours before the public were admitted, hanging her works and getting the display boards just right. She had been attending the display for some time, talking to people, who seemed interested, but not willing to buy.

She left Catriona and her dad in charge of the display and went off to see the rest of the fayre.

When she returned, the painting of some flowers was missing. She was ecstatic when she discovered that it had been sold.

She was thrilled and for the first time her self-doubts started to ease. Encouraged by her family she spent the next few weeks seriously contemplating art as a career. In the end, she applied for the foundation of art course in Glasgow.

Years later, when she was visiting her parents' home in Dunmerrick, she was putting some blankets in an old chest. Something tucked down the side caught her eye. It was carefully wrapped in bubble packaging. She checked it. It was her painting of some flowers; it had been secretly bought by her dad.

Gemma could never quite bring herself to have a row with her dad about that deception. His purchase of her painting at that critical time in her life had given her the confidence to apply for the course at the School of Art and that in turn had started her down the track to a career as an artist.

CHAPTER TEN

ROBERT WALKER

None of us can avoid the sweet pains of the sting of love.

Eileen Terry, *Love and other Foolish Things*, 1957.

Time inevitably passed on. Richard Graham Mackenzie Stansfield was still serving his jail sentence at Bowhouse. Gemma obtained her place at the Glasgow School of Art, where her outstanding talents were not only recognised but greatly encouraged. She started letting her hair grow long again.

Catriona pursued her own dream of taking a law course at the University of Glasgow. She also found love. She met Fraser Macintosh at a rather boring social function which neither had wanted to attend, but they got on well, soon started dating and after a whirlwind romance they were married.

Her mum and dad worried at first that she was getting married too early in life and too soon in her relationship, but they quickly accepted Fraser as a good future son-in-law. Gemma, as Catriona would always have expected, was 100 per cent supportive from the start.

The wedding was a wonderful affair. Catriona looked spectacular. Only one incident blotted Catriona's most special day. A cousin arrived with her new boyfriend. He walked with a slight limp and the shape of his face was similar to Stansfield. Most of the other guests had never heard of Stansfield, but the resemblance was striking to Gemma and Catriona. The shock of seeing him brought a flood of horrible memories back to Gemma and she fainted. Everyone else put it down to the heat, the excitement and the exhaustion caused by the tireless work that Gemma had put in to help make her sister's special day perfect. The scars of Gemma's abduction and rape had not fully healed and Catriona knew that her sister still had a long way to go to exorcise the devils in her mind.

Catriona moved out of the family home and for the first time the girls spent a lot of their time apart. Gemma still kept her Mood Wheel, which now had a curious mix of emotions represented all around it.

Fainting had prompted her to add 'attack' but it was only a single word score. Catriona leaving to set up home with Fraser, led Gemma to add 'alone' on a triple word space.

Gemma also kept her Sister Stuff cabinet in her art studio, which was now moved from the Art Shed into Catriona's bedroom. It was a little odd that even with her studio indoors, Gemma still referred to it as her Art Shed (1).

From time to time when Catriona visited Dunmerrick, the girls mulled over their plans of what to do when Stansfield was released from prison. Ideas of revenge were still very much alive.

Gemma was thrilled to bits when she won one of the art school's many competitions. She had been trying various forms of art. Her attempt at book illustration emerged as a winner.

So she was given the text of a planned children's book called *The Children of Wellwood Forst* and asked to produce some ideas which, might be used to illustrate it. She took her portfolio of paintings to the offices of the publishing company and was introduced to Robert Walker, who was putting the book together. Gemma had been left to decide on her own just what sections to illustrate.

"I did this one of the magpies," Gemma explained to Robert, "just because I liked what the author said, "It has to be a seven magpie secret.' You know from the rhyme, Five for silver, six for gold, seven for a secret never to be told."

"Yes, I liked that too... love your magpies. You've really captured the cheeky look of their characters."

"And this is the snake with an evil looking grin. Again it was.... well, I loved the bit about, 'The snake silently slinked stealthily through the grass.'"

"Yes, it's got some nice phrases. And some of the characters lend themselves to be illustrated."

"Oh, yes," Gemma commented, hardly listening but passing another painting to Robert. "This one is of the owl, you know the 'foul owl with the faulty howl'". And this one, well this is right at the start when the kids are standing round the bonfire they made."

"Oh yes..." Robert took it from Gemma and studied it for moment.

"I love the way you have the view from behind the kids and just shown their backs. Very unusual, but it works well. And this girl ... we have a side view of her. That's great. Wait a minute. That's you isn't it?"

Gemma blushed slightly and smiled. "Well, yes and no."

Robert enthused about Gemma's paintings and told her he thought she was a great artist. He casually chatted about Gemma's work for the book and what other kind of art she produced.

As she left Gemma couldn't help thinking that Robert was quite a nice guy. He had been so easy to talk to. He was a good listener. She had not had positive thoughts about any man since.... And she tried to push Robert out of her mind.

But no matter how hard she tried, Gemma could not quite get Robert out of her head. When she returned to her student accommodation she did what she usually did when her mind was buzzing with ideas or was in some form of conflict. She sat by the mirror and had a silent conversation with her reflection.

"He was actually quite cute."

"He's a man."

"He had a sweet smile."

"All men want just one thing."

"He didn't even notice me, not as a woman, just as an artist."

"What do I care?"

"DO I care?

"I don't know."

"He made me laugh."

"He's a man."

"Why am I even thinking about him?"

With that, Gemma went to bed and with a supreme effort pushed Robert Walker to the recesses of her mind.

It was a fine warm day between spring and summer. The air was still and there were only faint wisps of pale clouds in the sky. Gemma was in Dunmerrick to visit her parents and for the Culture Week events.

Dunmerrick was always a fun place to be during the annual Culture Week. There were exhibitions and performances at the castle, in the Curdie Art Gallery, the parks and at other venues. Street performers and buskers entertained passers-by with songs and shows. The lampposts were decorated with baskets of colourful flowers and the shops and cafes vied with each other to put on the most entertaining window displays.

The emphasis was not just on culture, but on fun. For the last few years, many of the shops had opted to have life-sized knitted figures in their windows, usually, but not always, relating to their business. Sputniks, a popular retro 1950s-1960s café had the Beatles on one side of their window and Neil Armstrong stepping on to the surface of the Moon at the other end, all knitted by Molly McVie.

One year Simon Semple had got into trouble when he painted the letterbox at Market Square in Saltire Blue instead of the traditional red. Although, for Simon, that had been not just a little bit fun, but a political statement.

Gemma was in the Market Square where some performers she'd been watching had just finished a puppet theatre production. Gemma had taken some photographs. She thought they might inspire her to produce some new works of art.

She was just wondering what to visit next when a familiar figure passed. It was Robert Walker. He paused and hailed her.

"Oh, hello," he called jovially, "It's eh, em Gemma, Gemma the artist isn't it?"

"And you are Robert, Robert the publisher?"

"Well, not quite. I've been meaning to call you. I might have some more work for you."

"That would be good."

"Do you want to get a coffee?"

"Ok," Gemma agreed. "Which one?"

They were just outside two side by side cafes, both, as it happened, run by the same family. Sputniks, the 1960s style diner had furnishing of tubular steel, framed with imitation red leather. All the food here was freshly cooked to order and the place was popular for meals and snacks.

Next door was the popular ice cream shop called An Ice Café. They chose the ice cream café. The warm weather had made the place busy, but Gemma and Robert managed to find a table near the door.

The counter, tables and chairs were all painted in soft pastel colours. The shelves along the walls were of pale green, but in sharp contrast the jars of sweets, boxes of cakes, biscuits and other goods stacked up on them had bright packaging, mostly of rich primary colours.

Robert was tall and slim without being gangly. He had long and rather untidy fair hair and, Gemma noticed, light brown eyes.

A couple of young girls in candy pink uniforms were busy serving customers. A middle-aged lady with a broad smile came over to them.

"Hello, Gemma. Good to see you back in town. How's your mum and dad?"

"They're fine. And your dad?"

"He's great. Trying to live in retirement. My brother's running the shop, but dad still helps out quite a lot."

"This is Robert. Robert, this is Rosemary Caine. She and David run the café. Her dad has a newsagent's shop."

"Hello Rosemary."

"I don't get called Rosemary much. Ever since I married David, everyone's called me Sugar. Sugar Caine," she added unnecessarily.

Gemma ordered a coffee. Robert's eye was caught by a poster advertising Capaldi's ice cream: *Made in Dunmerrick*. He ordered an ice cream deluxe.

"Well," Robert began hesitantly, as Sugar left hem alone, "As well as doing some editing work I also write my own children's stories..."

A lady in a wheelchair was approaching the door to leave the café. Robert got out of his seat to hold it open for her. He was back at his chair in a moment.

"... and poems, and I sing in a folk band; play the banjo."

"Is that why you are in Dunmerrick? Singing for the festival."

"Yep. We had a gig up at the castle this morning. It was really good. We have another one at Drouthy Tam's tonight. Do you know what they have in the dungeons at the castle?"

Gemma could not think where this conversation was going. "Eh skeletons, prisoners?"

"No. Spiders. Cathedral spiders. Big cathedral spiders... very unusual for this part of Scotland. It inspired me to start writing the story of Bruce and the spider, but for children. It's not finished, but I've made a start. Want to hear?" He pulled a notebook from a pocket and started to read from it.

"There's no' mony weans that like spiders. Come tae think o' it, there's no' mony audults like spiders either and the mair muckle the spider, the mair frichsome it is.

"But dae ye no ken that it wis a spider that helped a king tae mak oor land o' Scoatland.

"There's some folks will say that this is a true story.

Aye, weel, maybe it is an' maybe it isnae. It disnae really matter fur either wey, it's a guid wee story.

Gemma looked impressed. "You sound like my grandmother."

"I'll translate it into English later. Most publishers don't like stories in traditional Scots. Maybe I'll have two versions… one in Scots and one in English.

His enthusiasm was rubbing off on Gemma and while he had been reading Gemma had been studying him. He had a set of pairs of lapel badges; Yes and No; Up and Down; Left and Right; Soft and Hard, Right and Wrong.

It reminded her of her Mood Wheel that she had not added anything to for a long time. The word 'exciting' floated into Gemma's mind.

She commented on the badges and said that they should be Left, Wrong; Right, Right.

"Right, Right? Right." Robert commented with a smile," I collect badges, but only badges with one word on them. I must have a hundred of them," and seeing the look on Gemma's face, quickly changed the topic to something less boring.

"I'll move them around." He reached for one of the badges… "Ouch!"

"Pricked my finger" he said a mock childish voice, and a sulky look, before putting his sore finger in his mouth.

"Don't like pain. Look, one ear pierced." He pointed at the ear he had had pierced. It had a small dolphin decoration in it.

"That was sore." He pointed at the other ear, the one that had never been pierced.

"One was enough."

He smiled sweetly. Gemma returned the smile, but she was thinking all sorts of things, even as she laughed with him about this sore finger.

This guy is a complete woose. He's a child and he needs a good woman to dress him properly.

Gemma tried hard to push such thoughts out of her head.

"So you write your stories out in longhand," Gemma commented, looking at Robert's notebook and pen.

"Well just some notes and ideas, but, yes, I am very old fashioned. I use a phone to make phone calls, a camera to take pictures and a notebook to take notes."

"So what stories have you been writing that you would want me to illustrate."

"I've been writing about the adventures of squirrels who live in a country park."

"Squirrels?"

"Well, that's just one thing. I'd like to write a space adventure set in the future with people wanting to return to the earth because it's the home of their great grandparents. Something like that anyway.

"I try to write something every day even if it's only about the weather. All it takes is some idea to start me off, something I see or hear. Say something, anything."

Gemma knew well the idea of taking something at random and tuning it over and over in her mind until it provided some inspiration for her art.

"Eh, pirates," Gemma suggested taking the first thing that came to mind. One of the characters in the puppet show outside had been a pirate.

Robert paused, stared blankly for a moment and with a very theatrical voice began… "Jolly Roger was the most handsome pirate on the seven seas." He passed his hand over his own face and he revealed a roguish grin and twinkling eyes.

Gemma smiled. "No… " She announced sternly. "He's em, a retired pirate. He's now a school teacher," she invented wildly.

"Right then…" Robert thought a little more and in a serious tone came away with, "Mr Roger is just like any other school teacher you will ever meet, but Mr Roger has a secret. Have you ever wondered why everyone calls him Jolly Roger? It's not because he's always happy. Mr Roger used to be … a pirate."

"That's good," And in a commanding tone while stabbing the table with her finger, she added, "Write it down,"

"I will. I will." In his mind Robert thought, *'Don't nag'* but he was more amused than annoyed.

"When I make notes, I am never sure how they will be used until they have been thrown together, mixed up and left to simmer.

"I've got dozens of ideas in my head all fighting for my attention," he casually added. "I save as many as I can by writing them down."

Gemma's mind was in turmoil. She found Robert interesting, exciting, funny, friendly. Her eye was drawn to his left hand... no wedding band on his ring finger. Her mind was drifting to places she did not want it to go. And still he did not seem to have noticed her as a woman. At least, that's how it seemed to Gemma, but Robert's eye had already been drawn to Gemma's left hand too... no ring. His mind was also in turmoil and quite suddenly his confidence seemed to take a sudden knock.

In a rather nervous and flustered voice he made a suggestion. "We, eh, we should meet again to discuss, eh, you know, illustrations for the stories and things. I could, you know, take you out for dinner or something."

There was a pause before Gemma tentatively asked for clarification. "You mean ... on a date?"

"Well, yes, if you like." He smiled sweetly and hopefully.

"I, eh…" Part of Gemma's brain was already in panic mode. The other part was fighting hard to suppress the panic. The other part won and Gemma said, "All right."

Gemma was back at her parents' home before them. They were out enjoying the festival events too. Gemma was still a little flushed. For years she had shied away from boys, had deliberately tried to make herself less pretty, less interesting… and now, she had a dinner date with a guy who was, well, just so many things. She looked in the mirror thinking about her whirlwind of a day. She had to phone Catriona and tell her all about Robert

She reached out to pick up her phone but it rang just before her hand reached it. It was Catriona.

Gemma voice was full of excitement. "Hi Cat I was just about to phone you. I have some interesting news…. Oh good. Well, you go first…. What? WHAT? Cat, I'm on my way. I'll be there as soon as I can."

With tears sparkling in her eyes and a with a huge smile, Gemma took a moment to tell her reflection, "I'm going to be an auntie."

For that moment, and only for that moment, Robert was pushed out of Gemma's mind.

For the next few days Gemma was torn between excitement over her forthcoming date with Robert and terror, based on the memories of her ordeal at the hands of Richard Graham Mackenzie Stansfield. Catriona was a powerful influence and pushed as hard as she dared for Gemma to relax and enjoy her date. She even offered to be there, discretely in the background, but in the end Gemma's positive self won. She dressed in her most stunning outfit, made herself as beautiful as she could and set off to meet Robert at the Merchant City area of Glasgow.

They had chosen a rather nice Italian restaurant. Robert was dressed smartly for the date, well, smart for him.

They were both quite nervous. They casually talked about the menu and about the weather. Without saying anything to each other at the time, they were both horrified. They were talking about the weather. A waiter took the order. Vegetarian lasagne for Gemma; pizza for

Robert. Giving his order Robert asked, "I know you usually cut your pizzas into eight slices, but could you just cut mine into six slices, I don't think I could eat eight today." He sounded serious.

The waiter smiled obligingly and promised to pass the request on to the kitchen. As the waiter left Robert softly giggled, Gemma was laughing too.

"You're a little bit mad, aren't you?"

Robert feigned his annoyance. "No I'm not." And after a brief pause, he added, "I'm completely bonkers."

They talked about many things including possible work for Gemma. They exchanged ideas about art and for stories each seemingly trying to outdo the other.

"What about," Gemma suggested, "a place called Heron Knowe?" Robert obligingly wrote it down.

"And what if," she added at random, "the Hokey Cokey really is what it's all about?"

They had finished their meal. Robert suggested ice cream and Gemma who was having a lovely time in Robert's company agreed. She wanted the evening to go on and on.

"Well," Robert suggested with his roguish grin, "The best ice cream café is in Largs."

"That must be more than 20 miles away. You want to have a two course meal in two different restaurants 20 miles apart?

"You think I really am mad."

"No, actually I think it's a very romantic idea. It's completely mad, but it is romantic."

"Thank you."

CHAPTER ELEVEN

REVENGE

Great minds make plans. Great men carry them through.

William Martin, *Plans and Plots*, 1974.

Time moved relentlessly on, but Gemma and Catriona remained focussed on events of the past, despite the fact that for both of them life had moved on.

Gemma and Robert were married and found a lovely home called Ferrybridge House. Robert used part of the ground floor for a music studio and Gemma had space for an art studio which she continued to refer to as her Art Shed.

Robert's music studio was in what he and Gemma loved to call the east wing of the building. It was immaculate. Everything he used in the studio had a place and everything was always kept in its proper place. Every surface was kept dust free, and free of any clutter.

Gemma's Art Shed in the west wing, was in a permanent state of chaos. The walls were not adorned with finished works or works in progress. Such pieces of art were stacked up and left leaning against the walls. The walls were decorated with painted memos and slogans such as 'Ink makes you think, but paint makes you faint' bits of sketches, like a digital clock, which instead of numbers had E N D on the display, and various splashes of colour tests. The surfaces of a display cabinet, a table and that of two shelves were all cluttered with brushes, paints and a wide variety of nick knacks that Gemma used as props or for inspiration. Attached to the wall furthest from the door, but in view of anyone coming in, there was a dartboard with words attached. Those who did comment on it, tended to think that it was an interesting piece of art.

Even the spider web on the window was left alone as Gemma felt that the intricate pattern the spider had made might inspire her to produce interesting art. Gemma liked to use what she called the 'the hand system'. Everything she needed for her work was near at hand.

Despite all the jumble, the chaos and the apparent mess, it all somehow fitted together. It all looked as if it formed a whole. It seemed to be, in a sense, artistic. The only thing that appeared to be out of place was a steel grey cabinet in the corner. It had no clutter on it. It had no colour dabbed on to it, nothing attached to it, except one label that read Sister Stuff.

Gemma and Robert earned some extra income by hiring out studio time and giving art and music lessons. They had a good life. They had just about everything they wanted, except the one thing that they both craved more than anything else... a child of their own.

Catriona's family was growing. She had two young girls to look after and she had full time work with a law firm called Wright and McCourt. Things had never been better for Gemma and Catriona. And yet, niggling away in Gemma's mind was a memory that was impossible to forget, an incident that Gemma found impossible to forgive, and despite her legal background, Catriona was still the pillar of strength that Gemma needed whenever illegal plots of revenge were in her mind.

Then Richard Graham Mackenzie Stansfield was given early release from prison. He went back to Dunmerrick to live with a great aunt who was in the final months of her life, having been diagnosed with a particularly aggressive form of terminal cancer.

With the news that Stansfield was a free man, Gemma and Catriona opened up the Sister Stuff cabinet and started reviewing everything they knew about him. Catriona used some of her legal contacts to find out about Stansfield's time in jail.

It seemed that while serving his sentence Stansfield was bullied relentlessly by other prisoners who despised him. Child rapists were not ordinary prisoners like thieves or other criminals. He was threatened and he was assaulted; a kick in the ankle; an elbow in the ribs, a trip on the stairs. And he had to endure other bullying like someone sneezing over his food.

Although there had been no specific death threat, Stansfield felt that his life was in danger. There was no point in going to the guards or the prison staff. That would have made things even worse. Stansfield, however, did something just as drastic. He found the biggest bully in the place and went to speak to him. His story was that he was not a child molester. It was not his fault. He was a victim of circumstances.

In effect he told the prison bully, that he didn't know that the girl was just 15. She had told him she was 17 and he had no reason to doubt it. She was the one who wanted to go away for a couple of days. So, because she was under 16, Stansfield claimed, he was accused of raping a child. Because she wanted to go away and he took her, he pleaded, he was accused of abducting her and of course, Stansfield invented, the girl was well connected. Her parents had money and influence, so the court listened to her. "I never hurt her. I never hit her. This has ruined my life." And it seems that Stansfield, almost in tears, told his last hope, "I just thought you should know before someone in here kills me."

Stansfield's tactics worked. The word went out and the bullying stopped. Once again Stansfield actually came to believe the alternative version of reality that he created for himself and in this case it paid dividends.

Gemma decided that for a few weekends she would move back to Dunmerrick to paint some of the local landmarks. Robert was all right with this as he had some intense recording work to do.

Gemma cut some corners with some of the landmarks. She photographed the Curdie Art Gallery, Foley's Folley, the Freedom Monument and other local places of interest and painted them from the photographs. But she wanted to paint Glenbank Cottage, not from a few photographs, but by observation. She happened to know that there was an ideal vantage point called Poets' Tryst.

Poets' Tryst sat on a gentle rise above the main road. It was a popular starting place for people who wanted to take a walk through Dunmerrick Glen. It was a popular picnic place as well. The car park was well kept and the path to the glen and the car park borders were carefully planted with wild flowers. Poets' Tryst also overlooked Glenbank Cottage on the other side of the main road.

Gemma set up her easel and canvas board, but as well as her paints and brushes she had binoculars, a camera with a powerful zoom lens and she was ready to take extensive notes.

She carefully noted such details as she could of the house and the garden. The cottage was surrounded by a rather untidy garden. The walls were grey and looked as if they were in need of attention. The guttering also looked neglected. Gemma wondered if Stansfield had been concentrating on looking after his aunt and had not had time to get on with the tasks needed to keep the place in good order, or if he really did not care. However she had no answer to the question.

The condition of these parts of the house was duly noted. Gemma's first time sitting up there in Poets' Tryst was a month after the old lady had died. Stansfield was now living alone, which suited the plan that Gemma and Catriona had started to cook up.

She noted where he kept his rubbish bins and when he arrived from doing his shopping. She noted details of his car and from the bags he took from it, which supermarket he had been to for his shopping.

She already knew that Stansfield had a job with a garage a few miles away and she and Catriona had also hatched a plan to deal with that but only at the right time.

In the four hours that she had spent at Poets' Tryst that first day, Gemma had taken several photographs and had logged some new information, which was all collated and placed in the Sister Stuff cabinet. She also made a rather good start on a painting of Glenbank Cottage.

On her next two visits to Poets' Tryst Gemma did not get much in the way of new information, though she did make excellent progress on her painting. Although this was a bit of a distraction, Gemma was pleased with the work.

Then on her next visit something happened that changed everything.

Stansfield came out of the house and drove off. Gemma knew that he would be away for his weekly shopping and would be back in an hour or so. The change was so subtle she nearly missed it. Something in Stansfield's movement had been slightly different. She fished out her binoculars and scanned the front of the house. Even now she could not be sure, but it looked like he had left the key in the front door. Gemma packed quickly and set off. Yes. The key was there. Could she make it into town, get a copy of the key made and get back before Stansfield returned? She would have to risk it. Gemma drove into Dunmerrick, went to Allsorts ironmonger's shop and had a copy made. She hurried back to Glenbank, returned the original key to the lock where it had been left, then rushed across the road to the car park at Poets' Tryst, where she sat in excited anticipation, her binoculars to hand. As it happened, she had plenty of time. For some reason Stansfield had been delayed, and from what Gemma saw, Stansfield had no idea that he had left the key in the door until he returned home.

Now Gemma needed a new timetable, one that would allow her to be at this place when she knew Stansfield would be out of the house for most of the day. Fortunately Stansfield's work at the garage was made up of regular hours. The girls knew exactly when Stansfield would be at work.

Gemma was ready for the day of her new timetable. She parked at Poets' Tryst and as soon as Stansfield left the house, she made her way down the short flight of steps that led to the footpath along the main road. She crossed and turned into Stansfield's front garden. She had only a vague idea of what to do on this first incursion, but she wanted photographs, lots of photographs. As soon as she turned into Stansfield's driveway she was out of sight, hidden by a hedge. With a slightly trembling hand she took her copy of his key and gently inserted it into the lock. She turned and pushed. The door opened easily. Gemma stepped inside, but a moment later the emotion of memories of Stansfield's other home overwhelmed her. She withdrew, turned to the side of the house and vomited into the bushes. It took a moment to compose herself. She tried again and this time she was stronger. She once again penetrated Stansfield's private world. She took general photographs of each room to help build an image of the whole layout of the building. She took photographs of the contents of shelves, cupboards and the fridge. She wanted to know what products Stansfield bought. She checked the rubbish bins for anything that might later be interesting and although she had only been in the house for half an hour, it seemed like almost all day to her. As a final act of the day, and the first of what she hoped would be many acts of sabotage, she unplugged his refrigerator and put the electric kettle into its wall socket instead.

Gemma had spent a lot of time thinking about how and when she was going to tell Robert about what had happened in the past and about what she and Catriona were doing and planning to do. As it happened an opportunity arose a few days after she had first gone into Stansfield's house.

Gemma arrived home with some shopping. Robert was in the Thinking Room with the leather bound notebook that he used for ideas for stories and poems.

"Got any good ideas?" She asked him. "I've been looking at kitchen stuff. My head is full of pots and pans."

Robert grinned. "My head is full of plots and plans."

"Very good," she complimented him and in half serious voice demanded, "Write it down."

But Robert's mind was not on stories or poems. He told her that he had seen a mouse in the kitchen.

"That's not good," Gemma commented with a slight scowl on her face.

"I set Tramp on it."

"Oh no, that's cruel."

"That's nature. Well it would have been if Tramp had caught it. Do you know what that stupid cat did? It looked at the mouse, actually looked at it, then he curled up in his corner."

"So the mouse got away?"

"Ah wait, the story doesn't end there. I put some cheese out and guess what? Tramp got out of his corner and ate the cheese."

"Is this for one of your stories? Maddie the Mad Mouse. Tramp the scamp."

"No, it really happened. But, now you mention it, it could be a nice story. We would need to change the name of the cat to protect the guilty."

Gemma laughed. "Well mice don't like cheese. They like chocolate and peanut butter."

"So do I."

"Leave the mouse to me. I'll get one of those humane traps tomorrow. At least it will get a chance somewhere other than our kitchen. Do you think he lives alone?" Gemma was already thinking that she could let the mouse free in Stansfield's house.

Robert smiled. "That's it with you. You are so compassionate. You wouldn't hurt a living thing."

Gemma changed at once, as if she were controlled by the flick of a switch. She spoke in an unusually stern voice. "Well there are some creatures that are much worse than mice, or rats, much worse than any other animal vermin."

Robert was taken by surprise. This comment and Gemma's obvious bitterness was so unlike her. He gave her a quizzical look. Gemma returned a resigned sigh and started talking as though she had been rehearsing her little speech for a while.

"Robert, I like to think that we have an open, honest and loving relationship."

"We do."

"Don't interrupt. There is something I haven't told you, but it's time that I did."

Gemma told Robert everything. How, when she was at school she loved swimming and was very much a team player. How, just before she was 16, she was abducted and repeatedly raped. How her attacker was sent to jail but was now free. She told Robert everything she had done. How, even at school, she had obtained a copy of Stansfield's school record, how she kept news cuttings and she told him of the part Catriona had played and was continuing to play. She admitted to him how she was now watching Stansfield and his house and waiting.

She told him that she now had access to his cottage and that she was planning to do all sorts of things there in the hope that it would drive him nuts.

When she finished speaking Robert had tears in his eyes. It was so unlike him. Gemma had never seen Robert's eyes wet like that before. Robert edged closer to Gemma. He pulled her into a gentle hug. He stroked her hair, which by now was as long as it had been when she was a teenager.

"And only you and Catriona have been doing all this? Only you and Cat know?"

Gemma nodded. Tears were infectious. Gemma's eyes were wet too.

"Well," Robert said softly, "Now you have me on board too. I will do anything for you."

It was almost a month after Gemma had told Robert what she and Catroina were doing that the three of them finally got together. Catriona had decided not to tell Fraser and he had been left to look after the girls.

Catriona started by outlining much of what they already knew about Stansfield and his parents. How at school he was a slow learner. How he had always seemed to be what others felt was a borderline case, and how he drifted into petty crime and always seemed to need guidance from someone else, good people like his parents or bad people like Ben McCutcheon, but then, of course, his parents had been killed in a car crash.

When Catriona had finished talking, Gemma thanked her in what sounded like a rather formal vote of thanks, but this was not a formal meeting and there would certainly be no record, no minute of the meeting.

Gemma spoke next. She outlined mostly what she had been doing since she had gained access to Stansfield's house. She had replaced working light bulbs with dead ones. She had left milk and bread out and at other times had replaced fresh milk with sour milk and fresh bread with stale. She had taken the washed breakfast dishes and made them appear not to have been washed at all.

She had left electric heaters on. She had opened windows, taken cans and packets of food out of the cupboards and left them in the kitchen ready to be used. She had even replaced empty beer bottles with full ones, taking care to take away the empty bottles and even the bottle caps from the rubbish bin.

She had done anything that she thought would confuse Stansfield and make him question his own sanity. She had taken brand new bottles of shampoo, detergent and other things and replaced them with the empty bottles that Stansfield had put in the bin. She constantly unplugged and switched things off, and she had let a mouse loose in the house.

She had put some of the DVDs from Stansfield's huge collection in the wrong cases and she had taken some of them and placed them on the wrong shelf. And she had taken mail such as bills.

Robert had been listening carefully to the girls. Now he asked a few questions. Did Gemma know who supplied services such as water and electricity. Yes. Could she make an acceptable forgery of his signature. With a little practice, yes.

Then Robert added, "Do you know if Stansfield has any holidays planned? What I have in mind will need a week or two."

At the end of the meeting the three of them were excited. Curiously it was Gemma who now had a lingering doubt. When Robert went off to make tea and toast, Gemma quietly asked Catriona, "I suppose we are doing the right thing."

Catriona looked at her sister and reassured her, "We have to feed each other's sense of justice. Sometimes a path is laid out for you. You just have to know to take it."

CHAPTER TWELVE

ROBERT'S PLAN

The end is rarely the end. It is usually a new beginning.

Marshall Munn, *My Life*, 1938.

They were well suited to the task that they had set themselves. Catriona was quick-witted, analytical and able to anticipate problems and consequences; Gemma had that eye that was so important as an artist. She could spot things that the others missed. And it was Gemma who was set on revenge and was absolutely determined. Robert, the maker of stories, was imaginative and he was able to formulate an audacious plan that went far beyond anything that the girls had thought of.

Gemma and Catriona considered the questions Robert had just raised about Stansfield taking a holiday.

The momentary silence left Robert a little puzzled. "Well," he insisted, "where is it all going? What is your ultimate aim?"

Gemma repeated that what she was doing would make Stansfield question his own mind, which they all knew was not quite sound.

Robert pressed on with the idea that had been simmering in his mind, "But have you taken your plans far enough? I think you need to go further, much further. But to do that we need to know when he will be away for a while."

Robert ran through his plot with the girls. "It is vital that in our thinking and in our actions, we do not conform to what might be expected."

The plan he outlined was imaginative so outrageous that it might just succeed without anyone guessing what had happened to Stansfield, or more to the point, that anyone else had been involved.

They had a long wait. It would be three more months before Stansfield was planning to take a holiday.

But that was fine. It would allow them to get everything just right.

Regular raids on Stansfield's paper bin provided a treasure trove of information. They knew that for his holiday, he planned to take his time driving south, eventually arriving in London for a few days and then he would again take his time travelling back to Scotland. Stansfield was a great film fan. He had hundreds of films on DVD in the house.

In this waiting time the conspirators were not idle. Other parts of Robert's plan started to be put in place. Gemma stole a coat from Stansfield's house and she managed to pinch his driving licence which he never carried with him. She could only hope that Stansfield would not miss it. She continued her relentless campaign of sabotage and dirty tricks, like stealing all the spare rolls of toilet paper, moving the kettle from the kitchen to the bathroom, like causing a short circuit in electrical appliances and leaving food in the microwave oven as if it had been cooked ready to eat and he, Stansfield, had forgotten to take it out and eat it. She left windows open, lights and heaters on and she often went back to her first bit of trickery. She unplugged the fridge from the wall socket and put the kettle there instead. She left toast in the toaster. She left bags of shopping which Stansfield had not bought, in the kitchen ready to be put away. It was all the products that Stansfield usually bought.

They had no idea of the impact all this was having on Stansfield, but he had to be thinking that he was going shopping and then forgetting that he had been. No one breaks into a house to leave a bag of groceries.

Gemma learned to forge Stansfield's signature and she taught herself to write in his semi-literate untidy scrawl. She listed the utility companies he used and from stolen mail noted his bank account details as well as the details of his house and car insurance. Then with the help of Catriona and Robert, she compiled a series of letters.

Caution ruled. Whenever Gemma had been in the house she wore rubber gloves and she always had a cover story ready if anyone but Stansfield found her in the house. She had a key, after all. But no one ever did. Stansfield was a loner, with no friends and no relatives to visit him.

Whenever any of the three of them handled writing paper or envelopes or anything else that related to their plan, they wore gloves. Nothing was to be traceable back to any of them. All the letters had been written using a pen taken from Stansfield's home and when all the letters had been written, the pen was returned. Catriona said that modern forensics was very good, and this should be done, just in case something went wrong.

Gemma's car was frequently seen at Poets' Tryst but it was the only thing that was likely to link them to the site if, there was an investigation, and Gemma's art was a good cover story for it being seen there if the matter was ever raised.

Gemma's Sister Stuff cabinet was moved to Catriona's house. In the unlikely event of Gemma being the focus of an investigation, the secrets in that cold steel grey cabinet would be enough to send Gemma to jail.

Robert made sure that he would have the use of his band's van on the critical dates and he listed all the places that he and the others would need to visit after phase one of their plan had been completed.

The three of them went over every aspect of the plans time and time again, Catriona occasionally raising a point that needed tightened up.

Then Richard Graham Mackenzie Stansfield went on holiday, and the first of the letters was posted. It was an anonymous letter sent to Stansfield's employer and it contained copies of newspaper cuttings telling how Stansfield had been jailed for ten years for the abduction and repeated rape of a child.

Other letters were written, dated, signed, stamped and were ready to post at precisely the right time over the next few days. Nothing had been left chance. Everything had been carefully prepared for, planned and in a few cases, rehearsed.

The girls entered the house. Robert took a brazier round to the back garden. Their highest priority at this stage was anything that they thought could be traced back to Stansfield, anything personal, like an album of photographs of him as a child and of his parents. The photo album was one of the first things taken to the garden and chucked into the bonfire. To cut down on the volume of material they would have to drive away, they burned as much as they could. Packaging, papers, plastic items even some wooden furniture was broken up and burned. Everything small and combustible was burned in the brazier.

Most of the food that they found in tins, jars and cans was scattered in the back garden. It was picnic time for the birds.

All the liquids they could find, including shampoo, bleach, washing up liquid and even a can of beer were flushed down the toilet. If, for any reason, their van was stopped and searched, the cans and glass bottles would all be clean and empty and they would all be bagged, ready for recycling.

There were no books or magazines in Stansfield's house. He had hundreds of DVDs and they were put into more than a dozen carrier bags. Kitchen utensils, cutlery and crockery were bagged. Some clothing was burned, but most was bagged.

It took them two days to clear the house, not as long as they had expected, but in the end, the house was empty, completely empty. For the second time the van was full, completely full. Before they left, Robert took away the brazier from the back garden, and on Catriona's instruction, the ash from the two day fire was raked over and spread over as much of the garden as possible. Robert nailed a few boards carelessly (on purpose) over the windows and the front door. He placed a chain across the driveway and left a sign on the chain reading: Danger. Keep out.

Metal items such as cutlery, and glass bottles were dropped into recycling bins. Clothes and blanketing were dropped into charity skips. His furniture was taken to four different charity shops and Stansfield's vast collection of DVDs was split up and ended up in more than a dozen charity shops spread across a wide area.

Little by little, Robert had insisted. A van load of goods donated to a charity shop might raise suspicions, a single bag of goods donated to a charity shop would raise nothing but thanks.

Three days after Stansfield started enjoying his holiday, his cottage stood derelict and empty. Everything he owned, apart from what he had taken on holiday with him, was now either destroyed or scattered across the county in charity shops in half a dozen towns.

Nothing that had been passed on was traceable back to him and nothing was traceable back to the conspirators. And that was only phase one of Robert's plan.

Now the letters went out. The power company was told that the house was closed up and could they ensue that power was cut off permanently? A follow up phone call fixed a time and Robert met the men at the empty cottage to allow access. The water company received a similar letter and phone call and again it was Robert who met their representative at the closed up building.

These and the other utility suppliers were all told that arrangements were in place with the bank for final settlement of outstanding bills, as indeed they were. The bank had also been given written instructions in a letter in Stansfield's untidy scrawl and of course the letter had Stansfield's signature, or so it seemed.

Stansfield's house insurance was cancelled and to cap it all a building company was employed to demolish the derelict cottage at Glenbank. This was to be done as a matter of urgency in the interests of safety because of a serious structural fault which had been found in the building. Payment for the work was again authorised through the bank. They had calculated that there would not quite be enough in Stansfield's account to cover all the costs, but that account was topped up. It all went smoothly. It all went according to the meticulous plan. Of course it did. Every alternative, every possible problem had been anticipated and prepared for. Stansfield was in for a shock when he returned from his holiday. But the shock of discovering that his house was gone was just part of what Robert had planned for Richard Graham Mackenzie Stansfield.

They were waiting for him. They had been waiting for hours. It was starting to get dark when Stansfield drew up in his car. The chain was still across the driveway. The lopsided sign reading Danger: Keep out, swung gently in the breeze.

Stansfield got out of his car. He hadn't even turned the engine off. He stared at the danger sign and he stared at the blank plot. His confused mind was trying to take it in. "What the…" he muttered. There was a noise behind him. Someone had stepped into his car. It was moving away from him. He screamed, "That's my car, you bastard."

Almost at once another car stopped beside him. "You OK, mate?" The driver asked in a cheery but slightly concerned voice.

"That's my car. Someone just stole it."

"Get in. We'll catch them."

Stansfield clambered clumsily into the good stranger's car. And they followed the stolen vehicle.

"Can't you go any faster," Stansfield urged and the stranger muttered something about safe driving on a dark and twisting road.

"Right, now we've got them," the stranger told the distressed Stansfield. The stolen car had turned off the main road to the loch side road. This was a single-track road with passing places and occasional lay-bys at scenic or picnic points. The road ran the full length of Loch Marr, down one side and back up the other. It was about three miles in all for the round trip. There was nowhere else for a driver to go.

As Stansfield's excitement and anxiety grew, it was suddenly given another shock. His Good Samaritan pulled into a lay-by and stopped the car's engine.

"Get out," he unexpectedly demanded in a stern voice.

Stansfield, completely confused, stuttered, "Eh? What?"

He had not noticed that someone else had been in the car. From behind him a female voice added to the surprised confusion.

"You'd better do what he says. I have a knife and I'm not afraid to use it."

All three of them stepped out of the car.

"What do you want? What are you going to do?" Stansfield's time in prison had at least taught him to sound braver than he felt.

"Your jacket."

"What?"

"Take it off and give it to me."

Stansfield obeyed, while eying the blade of the knife in the woman's hand.

"Now your boots. Take them off." The three conspirators had felt that if they left Stansfield without shoes or boots it would slow him down considerably.

Jacket and boots were thrown into the back of the car.

"Empty your pockets." Stansfield did as he was ordered. "What's that in your shirt pocket?"

"My phone."

Robert took Stansfield's phone. "Well", he improvised in line with the plan, "You won't need that. It can go where your car is going." And he threw the phone into the loch.

"I think we're done here," Robert told Gemma.

But Gemma had another mind game to further confuse Stansfield. "You know, he might get really cold here. I think we should give him your coat."

Stansfield could not understand what was happening. The woman pulled a coat out of the car and dropped it at Stansfield's feet. They got into the car but before they left a frightened and confused Stansfield at the lay-by, she had one last message for Stansfield. In a sweet motherly voice she told him, "There are some sandwiches for you in one of the pockets and a beer in the other." She smiled sweetly at Stansfield and made a gentle laugh.

With that, she and Robert drove off down the side of Loch Marr. Stansfield watched the car until it was out of sight. He could not work out in his mind what had just happened. He did not know what to do next. Different ideas chased each other in his head, but none of them made any sense.

Then he saw them. Two sets of car headlights on the opposite shore of the loch. One of them had to belong to his stolen car. Quite suddenly the cars stopped and one pair of lights turned to face him. They dimmed and went out. The words about his phone echoed in Stansfield's mind. "It can go where your car is going." They had driven his car into the loch. For all the good it would do, Stansfield picked up a rock and threw it in the direction of the other car, screaming obscenities at those who had stolen his car.

The car, of course, had not been driven into the loch. The lights had been dimmed then switched off. It was only a couple of hundred yards in the light of the other car before they were out of Stansfield's sight.

The trio had rehearsed the manoeuvre several times and after careful observation, they knew exactly where to leave Stansfield and where to play this deception. The last part of Robert's plan was simple. Leave Stanfield's car, with the key still in the ignition in a place where it was most likely to be stolen.

All that remained was for Catriona to pull in a few favours to find out what had subsequently happened to Stansfield. It seems that he hobbled his way back to the main road where a kind-hearted motorist gave him a lift into town.

Stansfield went to the police where he told sceptical officers that someone had stolen his house and his car. The police were not quite sure how to take Stansfield. Was he a time waster or was he a bit simple? His story made no sense. Someone stole his jacket, but out of sympathy gave him a coat which not only had beer and fresh sandwiches, but also, just happened to have a wallet with a £5 note AND Stansfield's own driving licence. They checked what information they could, but as far as they could tell, the house at Glenbank had been demolished properly and with Stansfield's permission. The entire length of fencing round the loch was checked and there was no sign of a breach. No car had been driven into the water. The police were puzzled about Stansfield's car and simply added it to the list of stolen cars.

Then police spoke to a doctor who had been dealing with Stansfield for many years. She confirmed that Stansfield had a form of selective amnesia which gave him an ability to erase unpleasant memories and substitute alternative ones. It looked like Stansfield had suffered a terrible shock when he was told of the structural fault in his home and that it would have to be demolished. It all fitted. It was neat. It was clean.

Stansfield was in an advanced state of distress and confusion and he had nowhere else to go. He was found temporary supervised accommodation for the next few days but his condition did not improve. He was found a place at Craigmark Hospital, where his state of mind could be monitored and perhaps treated. The room that was available when Stansfield arrived there was the oddly named room 12A. It should have been room 13, but somewhere along the line a superstitious supervisor had decided to number it 12A.

That was it. That was their confession. They had told Mandy Stafford everything. She considered all that she had been told. She had taken many pages of notes. She had the story, a sensational story. But what would she do with it? What could she do with it? She could write a cracking good story for the paper, but it would surely destroy the careers of a talented artist and a promising lawyer. The bad guy in the story was dead. Mandy's mind was in turmoil.

As a woman who had dealt with other rape victims, Mandy understood exactly what Gemma, Catriona and Robert had done and why they had done it. It did not take her long to decide. She promised them that nothing would appear in print without their permission, and almost certainly not in the *Dunmerrick Herald*. Mandy was no longer thinking of a newspaper story that would make a ripple for a few days. She was already thinking of a book.

The final part of Gemma's recovery came later. After Stansfield had been in prison at Bowhouse for eight years, after he had been a patient at Craigmark for three years, after he had killed himself, after she and Catriona had told Maria O'Connell as much as they thought necessary at the time. It came even after she and Catriona had told Mandy Stafford, the truth, the whole truth and nothing but the truth.

Mandy went back to Gemma and Catriona with the outline of a book based on all that they had told her. It would be necessary to change the names of key people, places and institutions but it was, Mandy insisted, a story that had to be told in full.

The girls discussed it and talked about it for a long time, but it was Robert who persuaded Gemma to allow Mandy to go ahead with a book (1).

"Having your story written down like this might help heal your wounds, but it might also give other women who have been wronged a feeling that all is not dark in the world."

POSTSCRIPT

Robert was about to leave the house. He had a meeting with the representatives of a music publishing company and was dressed smartly for it. He was bubbling with excitement, but still sensitive enough notice a subtle change in Gemma's usual chirpy mood. As he kissed her lightly, he tenderly asked, "Are you all right, love? You seem to be a little out of sorts."

"I'm fine. Off you go. I think I'll put the finishing touches to the piece for Mandy's book. The publishers want it as soon as possible."

"Ah. I see. Well, don't get upset thinking about all that."

"I won't. I'll be fine. Off you go."

She pottered about, made a cup of coffee, deliberately delaying what she was about to do. There were only two possibilities. She had to do it now.

Gemma emerged from the bathroom. Her eyes were sparkling. Before picking up her brushes, she made some phone calls. She phoned Robert. She called Catriona and she phoned her parents.

She eyed up the work that she had done so far for the cover of the book that Mandy, with the girls' approval, had decided to call *The Dandelion in the Glass*. It showed, in reverse, a silhouette of a face, blowing the seeds of a dandelion head, in a pose that could have been blowing a kiss. Gemma loved the ambiguity. All Gemma wanted to do now was add a little red to the lips and the fingernails of the hand holding the dandelion. There was black background, white features, red highlights, and space for the title. Yes, that was shaping up nicely. She paused to switch on one of her all-time favourite pieces of music, *Wonderful World* by Louis Armstrong.

Gemma began working on the canvas. In the bathroom, the pregnancy kit she had left there read positive.

... Oh yeah.

ACKNOWLEDGEMENTS:

As a journalist I am always on the lookout for a good story. It is rare, very rare, for a journalist to come across what he or she considers to be a cracking good story and not to use it because of the probable impact on good people who, for various reasons, have taken the law into their own hands.

But stories like that tend to be too powerful to remain untold and that is the case with Gemma Dusk's story. The reader will appreciate that key names have been changed, to protect the identities of those involved in this case.

Although this book has my name on it, it is more than anything the story of Gemma Dusk. I spent many hours with Gemma and the others involved, checking and re-checking details, and I found Gemma to be a delightful and talented lady who is full of good humour. I can't praise her enough for the outstanding courage she has shown in reliving the nightmare that she went through. Thanks also go to her husband, Robert, and sister, Catriona, for their frank and honest contributions to this documentary.

There are other people and organisations I must thank. There is Maria O'Connell, of course. I must also thank officers of Police Scotland, Ayrshire and Arran NHS Trust and HM Prison Bowhouse and there are many other sources who do not want to be named. I also want to thank Flora Napier who acted as script editor. A few minor incidents have been related out of their correct historic sequence for better dramatic, or light-hearted, effect, but these are the only changes made to what really happened to Gemma and to Stansfield.

Don't be too quick to judge a young girl who was seriously wronged and a sister and a husband who love her, but ask yourself: *What would I have done?* What would you like to have done?

Mandy Stafford

Dunmerrick, Scotland, March 11, 2025

Notes on chapter 1

1: Ben McCutcheon continued his drift into petty crime. He died of a drugs overdose in 1999 at the age of 21. As the Dunmerrick Herald reported when his body was found in a back alley, 'There were no suspicious circumstances.'

2: What is popularly called Foley's Folly is not a folly at all. Set in Dunmerrick Glen this quaint little building with its water wheel was used to supply electricity to Broomhill House, the home of scientist and inventor, Maxwell Foley. He died in 1842 when his home was destroyed by fire. The isolated generating house remains as his monument.

3: The curious behaviour of a group of children scattering at the shout of the word 'hob' can still be seen in some rural communities in Ayrshire. It seems to have been passed down through many generations. Hob was an old name for the devil and it seems that at a time when people feared that the devil might appear among them the cry of 'hob' was enough to scatter them. Today's version of running away from something unpleasant seems to be an echo of that time.

Chapter 2

1: There was a change in ownership of the publishing company at this time and a change in policy. *The Children of Wellwood Forest,* remains unpublished.

2: Houses on the Witchcairn estate were built during the 1990s housing boom. The name comes from an ancient monolith believed to have had connections with witchcraft.

Chapter 3
1: From John Lennon's *Imagine.*

Chapter 5
1: John Curdie, 1821-1896, was an artist who gained considerable respect for the quality of his work, particularly landscapes. He had no formal training early in his career. Some of Curdie's paintings have found their way into public collections. Curdie eventually ran his own art school from his home.

2: The café was named in honour of Duncan McMillan, 1817-1866, a talented entertainer whose main acts included ventriloquism, impressions and singing. He toured all over the British Isles.

3: Loudoun Hill was the scene of conflicts between the Scots and the English invader during the wars of independence. The iconic sculpture by Richard Price commemorates conflicts of 1297 and 1307 and represents the spirit of the people of Scotland.

Chapter 6
1: At the time of writing this book there was a controversial plan in place to remove the footbridge and replace it with a wider road bridge to give additional vehicle access to Hudson Park. The park is named after Fergus E. Hudson, an early 19th century merchant who provided the land and the money for the park. He made his money from tobacco, and therefore, from slavery. It is ironic then, that the

people of 1890s Dunmerrick placed their anti-slavery monument in Hudson Park.

2: The red-haired girl was Sandi Forde, a cousin of Mandy Stafford. She had seen a vivid impression of a medal being awarded to a boy in a swimsuit. Even now she can't explain what happened. Sandi took a career as an archaeologist and has handled thousands of artefacts, but nothing like this has ever happened to her again.

3: Mandy Stafford has searched various sporting and other records but has never yet found out who William Kennedy was or what the medal was for. She now assumes that the medal is not local.

4: As things turned out the girls had laughed about this incident and the old popular song but when they were talking about the school's annual talent competition they thought it was perfect for them. They performed it in the school competition and came in second.

Chapter 7.
1: That image of Christ stayed in Gemma's mind for a long time and she eventually made brilliant use of it in a painting which won great acclaim from the art world.

Chapter 8
1: Former American slave, Frederick Douglass toured Scotland in 1846 at a time when slavery was still legal in the USA and there was still considerable political oppression in Scotland. Among other things he advocated votes for women. The Monument in Hudson Park was

erected by public subscription less than three years after the death of Frederick Douglass.

2: From *Tam o' Shanter* by Robert Burns.

Chapter 9
1: The flowers had not come from Molly McVie, but from Mary Bagtree's flower shop. She was in the habit of having her staff leave a bunch of flowers in unusual or interesting places with a note asking the finder to ensure that they were passed on to someone who deserved them.

Chapter 10
1: Gemma includes a dandelion in many of her paintings. Sometimes this is an obvious dandelion flower or seed head, but sometimes it is hidden, and often a single tiny dandelion seed is incorporated into her signature.

Chapter 12
1: In the months following the decision to produce a book, Mandy met Gemma and Catriona on many occasions. They became and they remain, good friends.

Printed in Great Britain
by Amazon